# THE RECKLESS DOCTOR'S BRIDE

## MONTANA WESTWARD BRIDES BOOK ONE

### AMELIA ROSE

# CONTENTS

*This book is dedicated to all of my faithful readers, without whom I would be nothing. I thank you for the support, reviews, love, and friendship you have shown me as we have gone through this journey together. I am truly blessed to have such a wonderful readership.*

# CHAPTER 1

*L*ucy couldn't tear her gaze from the staring, dark eyes of the dead man. His lifeless body lay face up on the ground, dried blood staining his dingy white shirt at the neck and across his abdomen. His long, curly, deep brown hair had bits of grass stuck in it and his tan, wide-brimmed hat lay close by, no doubt knocked off when he'd fallen to the ground after his assailant's attack.

"Lucy, go back to the buggy, and—."

The emotion-strained voice of her future husband startled her even though he stood right next to her. "What? N-no. I'm all right. I've seen dead bodies, just not with so much blood on them. I'm not squeamish, Sam." Bile rose in her throat, despite her claim, as she watched a fly crawl across Ernie's face.

Lucy looked up when Sam's hand settled on her shoulder. "I wasn't implying that you were. I just meant that we need to go back to town to fetch Sheriff Ryder. He needs to see this before Ernie's moved. I want to get back before scavengers disturb anything, or anyone comes along and moves him, or tries to steal his belongings."

Her eyes widened in disbelief. "Would someone really do that? Take his things?"

Sam's jaw tensed. "Yes. As you've seen, this land is still untamed. There are those who wouldn't think twice about stealing from a dead man."

Stifling the anger his response stirred, Lucy said, "Well, if anyone does, I hope they have nothin' but bad luck." She looked down at Ernie with a pang of sadness and regret before returning her gaze to Sam. "I'm so sorry for your loss, Sam, and I'm sorry I didn't get the chance to meet him."

Sam blinked his blue eyes and swallowed hard. "Thank you, Lucy." His voice was a trifle thick. "I know you would've liked each other."

Lucy gave him a tiny smile. "I'm certain we would've."

She followed Sam over to the buggy and waved away his assistance. Settling herself on the seat while he took up the reins, Lucy wondered who had killed Ernie and why. "Why would someone want to harm him?"

Sam's hands tightened around the reins for a few moments and a muscle in his cheek twitched. "I don't know, but I'm not going to rest until Ernie's murderer is brought to justice."

With a slap of the reins on the horse's rump, Sam put the buggy in motion. Lucy hung on to the seat as the buggy lurched forward, her heart thudding in her chest as she realized how dangerous this unfamiliar land could be.

It felt like she'd moved to the other side of the world instead of halfway across the country. The suddenness with which her life had changed in the short space of time since she'd come to Spruce Valley, Montana, alarmed her, and she wondered whether coming here had been a good idea after all.

*TWO DAYS EARLIER...*

*WHY DOES misfortune seem to follow me around, like a dark cloud hovering over my head?* It wasn't the first time Lucy Magee had asked herself that question, and she suspected that it wouldn't be the last.

Trudging along the muddy road, lugging one of her suitcases and her reticule, Lucy prayed that someone would come along to help her. She paused to catch her breath and a rivulet of sweat slid down her spine as she sat her suitcase down. The early June day had dawned, muggy after the heavy overnight rain, and the lack of a breeze made it even hotter.

Consulting her pendent watch, Lucy groaned in frustration. According to the timepiece, she'd have just been arriving in Spruce Valley, Montana to meet her prospective husband. However, her stagecoach driver had passed away while driving the conveyance about an hour ago.

As she'd been looking at the passing scenery, Lucy had noticed that the coach had started veering off to the right toward the edge of the road. She'd leaned her head out the open window and saw that they were approaching a bend in the road. Instead of the horses turning to the left, they'd trotted straight ahead.

Leaning further out of the window, Lucy had shouted to the driver but received no response. The horses had started to turn, but not before the right-side wheels of the stagecoach had slid into the ditch and gotten mired in the muck. Although she'd been bounced around in the coach, Lucy hadn't been hurt.

Once she'd gotten her bearings, she'd alighted from the vehicle and approached the driver's box. The elderly man had been slumped over and leaning to the right. As she'd gotten closer, he'd pitched forward and fallen off the coach into the ditch.

Horrified, Lucy had picked up the skirts of her powder blue traveling dress and rushed around the coach to his aid. However, as she knelt next to the man's prone form, his open, rheumy blue eyes told her that he was gone. Tears of sympathy and fear had slid down her cheeks as she'd closed his eyes with trembling fingers.

After saying a prayer for Mr. Trasker's soul, she'd taken stock of her situation. She wasn't a skilled driver, so she couldn't guide the horses in getting the coach unstuck. Thinking perhaps that she could ride one of them, she'd attempted to unhitch one. However, the scared horses wanted nothing to do with her and she'd left them alone after one had nipped at her.

Her only other option was to go for help. The thought of traveling alone along an unfamiliar road had filled her with trepidation, but she'd had no other choice. So, she'd chosen to take the suitcase with her most important possessions, and strike out for Spruce Valley on foot.

Now, taking out her handkerchief from a dress pocket, she wiped sweat from her face and then took a drink from the canteen she'd found in the driver's box. Her empty stomach announced that it was time for the midday meal, and she opened her reticule. She'd purchased a couple of Johnnycakes that morning before they'd gotten underway, and she unwrapped one.

She'd almost finished it when thunder rumbled overhead. With dismay, Lucy turned her gaze to the darkening sky and wanted to cry. Her luck just kept getting worse and worse. Gathering her things, she started hurrying along the road, determined to get as far as possible before she got soaked.

ALMOST SIX MILES AWAY, Dr. Sam Slater stood on the porch of Frost's Mercantile, which doubled as the stagecoach depot in Spruce Valley. He checked his watch and his brow furrowed with deep concern. Jed Trasker was the most reliable stage-coach driver in the southeastern area of the Montana Territory.

Sam knew something must've gone very wrong with Jed's run, because he could count on one hand the number of times the old man had been late. Not only was he worried about Jed, but also for the woman who was traveling all the way from Buffalo, New York to marry him.

He almost used the sleeve of his white dress shirt to wipe

sweat from his brow until he remembered that it was the best shirt he owned. It had cost too much for him to ruin it with a sweat stain. The ones under his arms were mostly hidden by his dark brown suit vest, which he couldn't wait to shed.

Once upon a time, dressing in anything except a full suit had been unthinkable when in polite society. Of course, that had been before he'd moved to Spruce Valley from Trenton, New Jersey three years prior in November of 1865. Montana Territory had only been signed into law one year before that, in May of 1864 by President Abraham Lincoln.

Most of the Territory was still wide open wild plains, which had appealed to Sam after all the carnage of the Civil War. As an army doctor, he'd seen more than his share of death and had struck out for the frontier, craving peace and desiring to help fill a shortage of physicians in the new territory.

He fished a handkerchief from his trouser pocket, mopped his sweaty brow, and consulted his watch again. Eleven forty-four, it read. His disquiet deepened, and he sighed. A loud, rumbling growl of thunder reached him and he hoped the storm would go around Spruce Valley. They didn't need any more rain after last night.

After another ten minutes had passed and still no stage-coach, Sam left the store. He crossed the dirt street, his booted feet sinking into the quagmire as he walked. Upon reaching the wooden boardwalk on the other side, he made his way past the small, squat clapboard building that served as his office and headed down the street to the newly built sheriff's office.

Entering the red brick building, Sam spied Sheriff Josh

Ryder—who'd been elected to office one month ago—sitting at his wooden oak desk. Josh looked up from the journal in which he was writing and smiled. "Did you bring your bride-to-be to meet me?"

Sam barely kept from running a hand through his sandy blond hair as his frustration mounted. "I'm afraid not. The stage hasn't arrived yet."

Josh's coffee-brown eyes filled with surprise as he looked at the clock on the wall opposite his desk. "Jed's never been this late."

"I know. I hope they didn't have trouble with robbers or Indians," Sam commented.

Josh closed his journal and got up. "Guess we best go find out."

Two other stagecoach drivers had recently had run-ins with robbers who'd stolen their cash boxes. Josh was working on catching them, but the thieves were smart and fast, making it hard for a law enforcement staff of only one to nab them.

Spruce Valley was located squarely in Crow Indian territory and every so often, they got riled up and caused some mischief. Of course, that was usually when they were warring with their hated enemies, the Lakota. When he'd moved to the area, Sam had been surprised to find that most of the Crow Nation was friendly toward whites.

So, although it couldn't be ruled out, Sam doubted that Jed had met up with troublemaking Crow warriors. In fact, many of the Crow in the area knew and liked the elderly man. No, something else was holding Jed up.

Sam said, "I'll go saddle Atlas and meet you back here."

"Fine by me," Josh agreed.

As soon as he stepped outside the sheriff's office, strong wind and fat drops of rain buffeted Sam, turning his mood even darker. He jogged back to his office and turned down the narrow alley between it and the wayside inn next door. The Honeywell Inn was a small establishment, boasting only four rooms for rent, but the owner, Bill Eckert, served good food and drink. He also employed a local widow, Greta Royal, who kept the place spic-and-span.

Reaching the livery stable behind the Inn where Sam boarded his horse when he was in town, Sam refused the stable boy's offer to saddle Atlas and did it himself. Swinging up on the big gray gelding's back, Sam trotted him outside and headed for the sheriff's office.

Josh was waiting for him, already mounted on a sorrel stallion. "Nice day for a ride," he commented with a wry gesture toward the sky.

Sam smiled and shook his head as the heavens opened, releasing a torrent. They turned their horses and headed east out of town. The bad weather on top of the missing stagecoach seemed like a bad omen to Sam. His anxiety intensified, and he urged Atlas into a faster pace. With a toss of his head, the powerful draft horse mix surged forward.

SODDEN AND MISERABLE from the deluge, Lucy sat on her suitcase. Her chin propped on a palm, she sat hunched forward, her elbow resting on her knee. She watched raindrops slide down a limp lock of her black hair that had fallen in front of her face.

Her right boot was stuck in the mud a short distance away and she'd placed her bare foot on top of her left boot, which thankfully hadn't been dislodged by the sucking mud. The thunder and lightning had died away, but the downpour continued.

Having looked around, Lucy had discovered that the area through which they'd been traveling was quite remote. There'd been no roads meeting the one upon which she'd been walking. No lanes, trails, or houses in sight either. Once the evil mud had stolen her right boot, Lucy had given up, plunking her suitcase down and sitting on it to wait out the storm.

A new sound caught Lucy's attention. Looking up, she saw two men on horseback approaching her. She almost stood up but remembered her bare foot at the last moment. Thrilled to see them, Lucy waved at them as though they were old friends she hadn't seen in months.

"Yoo-hoo! Hello!" she called to them.

Relief washed over her when the men stopped their horses close to her. It grew even stronger when she saw that one of them sported a worn badge on his rumpled black vest. Running into a lawman made her think that perhaps her luck was turning around.

Both men dismounted and the other one approached her with long strides. Looking over his tall, rangy form, her gaze encountered intense blue eyes set in a rather rugged face. One wouldn't call him classically handsome, but she thought his strong jaw, slightly crooked nose, and high forehead were much more interesting than the more refined features of some men.

His brows drew together, and she was touched by his concerned expression.

"Hello, miss. Are you all right? Are you hurt?"

Offering him a wan smile, Lucy replied, "Other than feeling like a drowned rat, being stuck in the mud, and stranded due to a nasty twist of fate, I'm just fine."

The smile that curved his mouth captivated Lucy. "I'm glad you're not injured and judging by that lilting Irish accent, I'd wager that you're likely my bride-to-be. I'm Dr. Sam Slater. Am I right? Are you Miss Magee?"

Lucy's heartbeat rapped against her ribs as excitement took hold of her. "I am! 'Tis surely Providence that brought ye along just when I needed ya most."

Sam held out a hand to her. "Well, Miss Magee, the conditions may be less than desirable, but I'm still very pleased to meet you."

Lucy slipped her hand into his. "And I am indeed thrilled to make yer acquaintance."

"Glad to hear it," Sam said. "Let's get you back to town out of this terrible weather, and you can tell me how you became stranded."

Sadness replaced Lucy's relief over being rescued and her smile slipped. "I'm sorry to tell ya that Mr. Trasker has gone to his great reward."

"Jed's dead?"

The man with Sam had asked the question and Lucy

turned her attention to him. "Aye. I believe that his heart gave out. The stage went off the road and got stuck. When I went to investigate what had gone wrong, I found him slumped in the driver's box. Then he fell off into the ditch. I went to assist him, but there was nary I could do. He was already gone, God bless his soul."

"I'm sorely grieved to hear this," the man said. "Jed was a good friend of mine."

"My condolences on yer loss, sir," Lucy responded.

His expression equally sad, Sam said, "Miss Magee, allow me to introduce you to Sheriff Josh Ryder."

Josh held out a hand to her. "Pleased to meet you, ma'am."

Lucy shook hands with him, thinking that he was also handsome in his own way. He had rather sharp features and wasn't as tall as Sam, but his brown eyes held warmth and intelligence. "Likewise, Sheriff."

Sam said, "Let's get going so we can get you settled, Miss Magee."

"Please call me Lucy," she said. "After all, we'll be married soon enough, and I don't see any need for formalities."

Sam nodded. "In that case, you must call me Sam."

"And call me Josh," the sheriff said.

Lucy smiled up at them. "Well then, Sam and Josh, I'm more than happy to get out of this swamp."

She held out a hand to Sam, who easily pulled her to her feet—or her booted foot, anyway. Josh retrieved her other boot and Sam steadied her while she put it on and tied it.

"There. That's better," she said.

"I'll take your suitcase and satchel, Lucy," Josh said. "I'm sure you'll want to ride with Sam."

Lucy's gaze left Josh to find Sam's eyes and she blushed at the twinkle in them. "Right."

"Sam, you mount up, and I'll help Lucy get up on that big galoot you call a horse," Josh said.

Sam cast him a dark look. "Don't make fun of Atlas." He swung into the saddle. "He's stronger than three other horses put together and twice as smart."

Josh chuckled as he assisted Lucy onto Atlas' back. She tried to hide her embarrassment at having to hike up her dress a little to achieve the task of mounting. It exposed a good portion of her calves and she adjusted her skirt to cover them more as soon as she was settled.

Looking down at Josh, she saw him glance away quickly, his face a little pink. She pursed her lips but said nothing. She supposed she couldn't fault the man for a little peek, but that didn't mean she had to like it. When she glanced at Sam, he turned around fast, but she knew he'd also been looking at her legs.

"I'll thank the both of ye not to ogle me so," she snapped.

"We didn't mean to, ma'am," Josh said. "It's just that I'm at eye-level with your leg and I sorta couldn't help it."

She glared at Sam. "And what's yer excuse?"

LUCY'S CHALLENGING tone both amused and shamed Sam. She had the right to be upset about strange men staring at her shapely calves, but he hadn't been able to help himself. It had been a long time since he'd had the company of a woman and Lucy was very desirable.

Even with her inky hair plastered to her head, her dirty dress, and a smear of mud on her right cheek, her beauty was undeniable. Her marvelous gray eyes were stormy with anger right now, and her delicate chin thrust forward in defiance and Sam thought she was the most beautiful woman he'd ever laid eyes on.

"I was just making sure you were comfortable and couldn't help seeing your legs since they're right there," he said. "I honestly didn't mean to offend you, Lucy."

She was quiet for a few moments and then nodded. "Very well, then. I believe ya."

Sam smiled and turned back around. He tapped Atlas's side with his heels and the horse broke into a trot. Lucy's arms came around his waist and his pulse jumped at the contact. He was glad she was putting safety above shyness and concentrated on the road ahead, shoving the way she felt against his back out of his mind as best he could.

# CHAPTER 2

*A*n hour later, Lucy reclined in a tub of hot water, washing the mud and grime from her skin with the jasmine soap that Mrs. Royal had brought for her. Although her room in the Honeywell Inn was a little stuffy, the bath still felt good. Since her hair was already wet, she decided to wash it.

Once she was done, Lucy finished up and dressed in her best dress from the suitcase she'd taken from the stagecoach. Luckily, it had proved watertight and her belongings had remained dry. She donned petticoats over her shift, along with a simple white corset and a white blouse. She finished the ensemble with a pink paisley cotton skirt. Her thick hair would take a long time to dry if she put it up or braided it, so she left it loose around her shoulders.

Collecting her beaded drawstring purse, she left her room and walked down the hallway to the stairs. The aromas of savory meat and ale made her stomach rumble almost as loud as the thunder had earlier. At the bottom of the stairs, she turned left into a large dining room in which five square tables stood.

Sam was standing by one of the windows with his back to her, gazing out of it. Lucy took in the breadth of his shoulders and the way his wavy blond hair curled over his collar. He turned around and she realized that he must've seen her reflection in the glass. Not wanting him to catch her staring at him, especially when she'd just chastised him for that offense, she pretended to look around.

"Hello, Lucy. Feeling refreshed?" he asked, walking toward her.

"Aye, thank you." She gestured at the room. "This seems like a lovely little place."

Sam smiled and motioned to the table she stood next to. "It is. Please, sit. Mrs. Royal is getting us something to eat."

Lucy let him seat her and sat her purse on an empty chair.

"Other than the very last part, how was the rest of your trip?" Sam asked as he joined her.

"Exciting, nerve-wracking, and very, very long," Lucy replied. "And not a journey I care to make again anytime soon, if ever."

Sam chuckled. "I remember making the trip and I felt the same way once I got here. Maybe in a few years, once traveling gets easier, you'll want to go back for a visit."

"Perhaps, but right now, I'm very eager to start a new life."

"Ah, yes. Ready to be free of all those siblings," Sam remarked wryly.

Lucy frowned. "I love them, well, most of them, but even if I had wanted to stay, Ma and Da were pushin' me to marry."

Sam leaned his elbows on the table. "Yes, you said as much, and I still find it hard to believe that there wasn't a single eligible man in the whole of Buffalo, New York who would marry you."

Lucy arched an eyebrow and lifted her chin. "Ye have that backward, Dr. Slater. There wasn't a single man I'd met in Buffalo *I* wanted to marry, so before my father picked for me, I took matters into my own hands."

Sam gave an understanding nod. "I think you did the right thing. I'd say that even if you hadn't come here to marry me. I'm more forward-thinking than some men and believe that women have the right to decide their own destiny."

"I gathered that from your letters, and it was one of the reasons I chose ya," Lucy said. "I didn't want to be trapped in a marriage with an overbearin' man."

"I have my stubborn moments, but I'd never hurt your feelings on purpose, Lucy. It's important that you know that about me," Sam informed her.

"Thank ya. I appreciate that."

Greta arrived with a large tray of food. The tall, thin woman gave them a warm smile that made her green eyes shine with good humor. "Here we are. Some nice roast beef, mashed potatoes, and green beans." She placed steaming-hot plates in front of them, along with glasses of lemonade. "And when you're ready for dessert, we have some nice custard pie and coffee."

Lucy's mouth watered as she looked at the food. "It all looks wonderful. Thank ya, Mrs. Royal."

"You must call me Greta." The middle-aged woman patted Lucy's shoulder. "Now, you just let me know if there's anything you need." She gave Sam a stern look. "And you'd better be good to this young lady."

Sam chuckled. "You have nothing to worry about, Greta. I intend to spoil her."

Lucy blushed and laughed when he winked at her.

"Glad to hear it," Greta responded. "I'll be back to check on you."

Lucy bowed her head and said a silent grace before tucking into her food.

SAM HID his amusement as he watched Lucy attack her food with gusto. He could imagine how famished she was after all she'd been through. After a few moments, he turned his attention to his own food, happily filling his own empty belly. As usual, the food Bill had prepared was scrumptious and it didn't take long for each of them to clear their plate.

After sopping up the last of the gravy from his plate with a piece of fresh bread, Sam sat back. A couple of minutes later, Lucy did the same thing and let out a sigh of contentment.

"The cook here is excellent," she commented.

"Yes, Bill is quite talented," Sam agreed. "I know you'll

want to rest tonight, but tomorrow I'd like to show you my ranch."

Lucy was eager to see the place she'd soon call home. From Sam's description in his letters, it was a beautiful piece of land. "Aye. I'd like that very much. When will we wed?"

"Is Sunday too soon?"

Lucy fidgeted a little and she seemed to mull that over. Finally, she said, "Sunday will be just fine. I brought my dress, so there won't be any need to shop for one or have one made."

Sam guessed at the source of her anxiety and put his hand over hers. "Lucy, we don't know each other very well yet. I don't expect relations on our wedding night. Before we take that step, I'd like to become better acquainted. My house has two bedrooms, so you'll have your own until you're ready to move into mine."

Her shoulders sagged and a relieved expression settled on her face as she squeezed his hand back. "I hope yer not offended, but I'm happy to hear that. I wasn't sure what yer feelings were on the subject."

Sam gave her hand a last squeeze and released her. "Well, now you know."

Greta arrived with their coffee and custard pie. They ate their dessert in companionable silence, enjoying the treat. By the time they'd finished, Sam noticed that Lucy looked fatigued.

"Lucy, why don't you go rest and I'll pick you up around eight tomorrow morning," he suggested.

She sent him a tired smile. "Aye, I'm quite tired and now

that my belly is full of such good food, I feel like I could sleep for a week."

Sam rose, and she followed suit. "Then I won't keep you." Moving closer to her, he took her hand, and brushed his lips over the smooth back of it. "Goodnight, Lucy. Pleasant dreams."

Looking into her slightly dazed eyes, Sam was certain a spark of attraction sparked between them, which pleased him. He walked her to the stairs where Lucy turned to him.

"Thank ya for everything," she said. "Goodnight, Sam."

He gave her a smile and a nod, and then took his leave.

WONDERMENT FILLED Lucy as she and Sam turned down the lane to his ranch the next morning. After growing up in a city, the vast expanse of farmland that spread out before them was a surprise to her. She'd gotten glimpses of fields and forests on the trip to Spruce Valley, but she hadn't yet seen a ranch.

A small one-story, white clapboard ranch house stood a little way down the lane on the right. A large red barn had been erected farther down the lane with wooden fencing running out from the back of it. Several horses grazed in the pasture and a couple of dogs came running toward the buggy.

A sea of prairie grass stretched out as far as Lucy could see, meeting the dazzling blue sky above the horizon. Maple and birch trees dotted the ranch and there was a white bunkhouse on the left of the driveway.

Sam's voice interrupted her thoughts. "I know it's a little

plain, but I left it that way purposely. Same with the house. I thought it would be nice to decorate it together, to make it ours."

His consideration touched Lucy. "'Tis a lovely piece of land, and I'm sure the house is, too." She gave him a teasing smile. "And I certainly don't mind giving the place a woman's touch."

His grin made her pulse skip. "It needs it."

He halted Atlas in front of the house and got out of the buggy. "You go on ahead and I'll start bringing in your luggage."

Lucy said, "Aye," as he helped her out of the vehicle. "I confess that I'm anxious to see it."

He gestured dramatically toward the house. "Then by all means."

As Lucy walked along the path to the porch that ran the length of the house, she envisioned the walkway lined with colorful flowers. She could also plant low shrubs in front of the porch. Stepping up onto it, she noted that the wide plank boards had been freshly painted a gray that matched the shutters and contrasted nicely with the white house.

The screen door was painted the same color, but the inner wooden door was white. Lucy liked the ornate brass doorknob and doorknocker. Opening the door, she stepped into a small foyer, which opened onto a hallway. The hardwood oak floors gleamed, and the walls had been painted a rich cream.

There were several doorways on each side of the hallway. The first one on the left revealed a large parlor with three tall windows. The weather had cleared overnight, and sunshine streamed through the glass, filling the room with warm light. A green-and-white floral sofa, love seat, and two wingback chairs were situated around the room facing the fireplace that stood between two of the windows.

Lucy envisioned her and Sam sitting in front of a roaring fire on winter nights. She would perhaps work on mending and he would read a book. A giggle bubbled from her over her daydreaming. She turned when she heard footsteps in the hallway.

Sam, lugging one of her trunks, halted in the doorway. "What do you think?"

"Well, I only got this far, but if the rest of the house is as nice as the parlor, I'm going to love it," Lucy replied.

His grin lit up his amazing eyes. "I'm glad to hear it. Well, I'll get this to your room."

Lucy followed him. "I'll come with you."

"All right."

As she walked behind Sam, Lucy couldn't help admiring his fine form. His broad shoulders tapered down to a trim waist and his trousers hinted at a nice backside. Her cheeks heated, and Lucy tugged her thoughts away from that subject.

The next room on the left was the dining room which led into the kitchen. Since Sam hadn't told her much about the house yet, Lucy was surprised to see that the sink had a pump in it. It would be much more convenient than having to constantly haul water from a well, especially on wash day.

Sam joined her in the kitchen just as she came out of the pantry and she commented on the pump. He said, "I'm glad you like it, but don't get used to it."

Lucy's brow puckered in confusion. "Why not? You're not after takin' it out, are ya?"

His lips twitched, and she knew that her Irish phrase had tickled his funny bone. "Well, I am, but only because a friend of mine who's a master plumber is coming from New York City next month to install indoor plumbing."

Lucy's mouth dropped open. "Indoor plumbin'! We didn't even have that back in Buffalo. Of course, we're rather poor, but still. Only the wealthiest had a water closet." She narrowed her eyes at him. "How can ye afford that?"

He leaned a hip against the counter and crossed his arms over his chest in a pose that pulled his shirtsleeves tight around his biceps. Those biceps, his slightly ruddy complexion, and strong hands showed that he was used to hard, physical work. He might be a doctor, but it appeared that he didn't spend all his days in an office.

"Mike Prentiss and I grew up together in New Jersey, but he left to be an apprentice with an engineer when our formal schooling was through. I helped him start his business and now he owes me a few favors," Sam replied. "He was out here last year and said the water table on my property was high enough to support indoor plumbing. So, you'll be the envy of Spruce Valley since no one else except Bill has it."

Lucy couldn't help being thrilled at the prospect of having such a modern home. She'd never expected to live in a place with running water. Not only that, but the cookstove was a newer, eight-plate model with a double oven, which meant she could cook more things at the same time. The pantry was large and very cool, despite the heat. Food would stay fresh longer in it.

Smiling at Sam, she thought she'd have married him for just the kitchen alone. "I thought ya were just teasin' about spoilin' me."

Sam straightened and stepped closer. "No, I was serious. After all, what's the point of having a beautiful woman if not to spoil her?"

The sudden heat in Sam's eyes sent Lucy's pulse galloping. His compliment made her blush, but she was determined not to be bashful. She was a grown woman of twenty-four—practically a spinster—not a young schoolgirl with a crush. And Sam was a very handsome man who seemed to find her attractive. It wasn't as though she'd never been kissed, and it seemed as though Sam had kissing on his mind.

Wouldn't it be good to know if they had any chemistry before they kissed at the wedding? Call her wicked, but Lucy didn't want their first kiss to take place in the presence of other people. As he closed the distance between them, Lucy's breathing grew shallow.

He raised a hand and cupped her cheek.

Suddenly, a female voice cut the quiet of the house. "Hellooo! Yoohoo!"

Sam frowned as he dropped his hand and took several steps away from Lucy.

"Dr. Slater?"

"In the kitchen, Mrs. Stavros," Sam called out.

Lucy gathered her wits as a plump, seventy-ish woman

entered the kitchen. Her dark eyes glittered with curiosity and a welcoming smile curved her generous mouth.

"Hello, Mrs. Stavros." Sam motioned toward Lucy. "Allow me to introduce you to my bride-to-be, Miss Lucy Magee. Lucy, this is Mrs. Delphina Stavros, my neighbor, good friend, and our mayor."

Lucy's eyes rounded as she gave Mrs. Stavros a small curtsey. "Pleased to meet you, ma'am. I've never heard of a woman mayor before."

"How do you do?" Mrs. Stavros greeted her in heavily accented English. "It's good to meet you, as well. My husband Anton was the mayor, but he passed away last year. No one else ran for mayor, so I took his place." She chuckled. "There are only around two hundred people in Spruce Valley, so usually, there is not much to the job."

Lucy said, "It's still impressive to meet a lady mayor. It gives hope that perhaps the rest of the people here are a little forward-thinkin'."

Mrs. Stavros sobered. "Some more than others. There are those who are not happy with a woman holding the reins, but I do not let them bother me."

"Whoever doesn't like it can go hang," Sam chimed in. "You're doing a great job and I hope you stay at it for a while."

A pleased smile lit up Mrs. Stavros' eyes again. "You're much too kind, Sam, but I appreciate your support."

Sam noticed that the older lady carried a large wicker basket and nodded toward it. "What do you have there?"

Looking at Lucy, Mrs. Stavros replied, "I must confess

that I became very curious when I heard that you'd arrived and just had to come meet you when I saw Sam's buggy pass my house." Sadness pinched her handsome features. "I can't believe that Jed is gone." She sniffed and pulled a handkerchief from her skirt pocket. "He was such a good man and a good friend. I'm going to miss him."

Sam put a comforting arm around her. "Me, too, but at least he didn't suffer. He's in a better place now."

Mrs. Stavros nodded and dabbed at her teary eyes. "Yes, you're right. Anyway, I knew you most likely hadn't thought about preparing lunch, so I put one together for you." She handed the basket to Lucy. "I thought Sam might take you to meet Ernie, so there is enough food in there for you all."

Surprised by the heaviness of the basket, Lucy thought that Mrs. Stavros must've packed enough for a small army. "How thoughtful of ye. Many thanks."

"That's what makes her such a great mayor," Sam said. "She's always thinking ahead."

Mrs. Stavros waved away his compliment. "I must get back home to help Elena with the children. My daughter has four little ones and they keep everyone stepping. Lucy, I look forward to becoming friends. You must come for a visit soon."

Lucy beamed, thrilled to make a friend. "I would enjoy that very much. Thank ya again for the food."

"You're quite welcome, dear," Mrs. Stavros said.

"I'll walk you out," Sam announced. "I'll be right back, Lucy."

"I'll be here," she quipped and watched them walk from the room.

SAM GLANCED at Lucy as he drove his buggy past the barn and headed for his sheep herder's camp. Her black hair, which she'd put up in a low bun that day, was hidden by a white cotton sunbonnet. It was saved from being plain by the pretty, swirling green and gold leaves that had been stitched around the brim.

He looked away from Lucy, facing ahead again. Try as he might, it was almost impossible to keep his eyes off her. Irritated by his immature behavior, Sam forced himself to be a good host instead of acting like an infatuated schoolboy.

"How long will it take to reach Mr. Red Dog's camp?" Lucy asked.

"The better part of an hour," Sam replied. "I'm glad it cleared off so we can make the trip. I wanted you to meet him and tell him about the wedding."

"Will he come to it, then?"

Sam smiled. "Ernie's not much for Christianity, but he'll attend just because I asked him to."

"Because he's an Indian?"

"Well, he doesn't have much Indian blood, just an Indian last name. His great grandfather was a member of a Crow tribe from this area," Sam said. "Ernie doesn't consider himself white, or Indian, or colored—just a man. And he doesn't have time for any religion or believe in *any* god."

"But he's still your friend?"

Some men might not like Lucy's straightforward, inquisitive nature, but Sam was enjoying it. Although she might not have had much formal education, through their correspondence, he'd learned that her Uncle Liam was an educated man who'd insisted on teaching his nieces and nephews as much as possible.

An avid student, Lucy had soaked up her uncle's lessons. As a result, she knew a great deal of mathematics, writing and reading, and history. Sam had been impressed by her intelligence and knowledge as much as he had been by her beautiful picture.

"Ernie is a good, honest man," Sam said. "He taught me everything I know about raising livestock and conducting cattle drives. When I first arrived here, I was surprised to find that there were so few people in town, which means fewer patients, so less income. I had to do something to make money. I became friendly with Ernie and he pointed me to my land.

"He grew up herding sheep, so when he offered his services as such, I took him up on it right away. He helped me put together a good herd and I made him my business partner. I take care of things around the ranch and he takes care of the sheep."

Lucy's smile drew his attention to her mouth, and he felt the urge to kiss her again.

"I'm glad that ya have such good friends," Lucy said.

Sam reached over and took her hand. "They'll be your friends, too. You'll see."

He enjoyed the feeling of her smaller hand in his and was glad when she didn't pull away. The back of her hand was smooth, but the light callouses on her palm proved that she was used to hard work. This was a relief to him because life in their remote, frontier area could be harsh and hard work was crucial to survival.

He lifted her hand and pressed a kiss to it. The blush that blossomed in her cheeks and the way her eyes darkened made him want to kiss more than her hand. Giving it a last squeeze, he let it go.

They chatted almost the whole ride, and Sam couldn't remember the last time he'd enjoyed a conversation so much. He was almost sad when they arrived at the sheep herder's camp because he didn't want it to end. With an internal chuckle, he reminded himself that he was going to have a whole lifetime to converse with the special woman riding beside him.

Nearing Ernie's camp, Sam grew concerned when he saw only a few sheep around the area. Normally, they were milling about, grazing or sleeping. Ernie's dogs, Chip and Millie, were nowhere in sight.

Swinging his gaze to the right, his disquiet deepened when he saw that no fire burned in the pit outside Ernie's shepherd's shed. No smoke rose from the small pipe sticking out of its roof, either.

Stopping the buggy next to the shed, Sam called out, "Ernie! Are you here?"

Upon receiving no response, a chill of dread crept up Sam's spine. He got out of the buggy and Lucy did the same. Sam walked toward the shepherd's shed with long, urgent strides, calling out to his friend. However, still no answer met his loud calls.

As he was about to open the shed's door, Sam noticed something out of the corner of his eye. To his right, peeking out from around the corner of the shed was a man's boot. But not just any boot. The sight of the worn, dingy, tan hide of a moccasin boot caused Sam's heart to leap in his chest because he knew it well.

Rushing around the corner of the shed, Sam found the body of one of his best friends. Sam fell to his knees beside Ernie and began assessing him, even though he knew that Ernie was dead…

# CHAPTER 3

 he Present...

"ARE you sure you won't bury him in the cemetery?"

Sam offered Reverend Paul Gibbons a tight smile. "I'm certain. I've finished my post-mortem examination and I'll take him to his sons. He once told me that's what he wanted if I outlived him."

Paul sighed and leaned back in his wingback chair. "Very well."

Sam stared into his sherry—the strongest drink served in the Gibbons' home—and then looked around the comfortable if sparsely furnished parlor. It wasn't mostly devoid of decoration or bric-a-brac due to religion, but because Mrs. Gibbons found that it made her housekeeping easier. The time she saved on such mundane chores as dusting and sweeping, she used in pursuing her true passion—music.

Sam's sadness thawed slightly when Mary's spectacular soprano voice swept up and down a scale, the sound carrying easily to them from upstairs. "Annette sounds in fine form."

Paul chuckled. "Yes, she does. The voice of an angel. What a pity that none of our children inherited even half of her gifts." He straightened again. "Are you certain that I can't even pray over Ernie or—"

"Paul, I know you mean well, but I won't go against Ernie's wishes and have him haunt me. I'll take his body out to the woods in the morning, as promised, and give him to his sons," Sam insisted, growing irritated.

Paul lifted a placating hand. "All right. It just feels so wrong to not do something for him."

Sam's anger abated at Paul's contrite expression. "You *are* doing something for him—what he wanted—and I'm sure he thanks you."

Paul nodded curtly. "Does Josh have any idea who might've done this?"

"Not yet but give him time. Josh is as dogged as any bloodhound and twice as fearsome as a bear," Sam replied. "Although, if I find out who did it—"

"You'll turn him in." Steel laced Paul's voice and filled his dark eyes. "Don't utter one more word of sinful intentions, Sam."

Sam's fingers tightened on the arm of his chair and he knew it was time to leave before his anger sharpened his tongue. He forced himself to relax and finished his drink. "My apologies, Paul. I'm just out of sorts."

"I understand how troubled you are," Paul said. "But don't let Ernie's death pull you into darkness again, Sam."

*I fear it's already too late.* Sam pushed that thought away and stood up. "You're right. I won't. Ernie wouldn't want that, and I have responsibilities and a lot to look forward to."

A grin lit Paul's craggy face. "Such as marriage to a fetching Irish lass?"

Lucy's beautiful visage rose in Sam's mind, and he couldn't stop his own smile. "Yes. I'm glad I picked her. She's intelligent, strong, and beautiful—exactly the kind of woman I wanted."

"I'm glad to hear it. You deserve to be happy, Sam."

Sam nodded. "Well, I have a little work to do before bed. Goodnight."

"Goodnight, Sam."

As Sam left the reverend's house, a breeze kicked up and an owl screeched from somewhere nearby, no doubt in search of a meal. Sam strolled along the walkway that ran from the parsonage along the side of the church to the main street. As he neared his office, he thought about stopping to see Lucy for a few minutes. She'd been going to spend the evening at Greta's, working on some sewing.

Deciding his paperwork could wait until morning, Sam cut across the street to the tiny house Greta called home. Normally, Greta was a frugal person, but she'd paid extra for the yellow paint that now covered the house. It was a warm, sunny color that brought to mind spring days and rays of golden light.

Sam mounted her low porch and knocked on the door.

Greta opened it and smiled at him. "Dr. Slater, to what do I owe the pleasure, as if I don't know?"

Sam chuckled. "Yes, I've come to see Lucy, but you know I'm always happy to see you."

"Ever the gentleman. Come in, please. May I offer you some coffee or tea?" Greta asked, showing him into her parlor.

Lucy looked up from her sewing. Her smile of welcome distracted Sam for a moment.

"Uh, yes, Greta. Whichever is easiest would be fine," he said. "Hello, Lucy. How is your work going?"

"Very well, thank ya," she said. "How are you doing?"

Sam took off his black Cutter hat made by a new company by the name of Stetson. It was a young enterprise, only three years old, but already word of their exceptional hats was spreading. When he'd accompanied Ernie on a cattle drive to Texas the previous year, he hadn't been able to resist buying it, even though it had cost him quite a tidy sum of money.

He sat in a straight back chair close to Lucy and rested his hat on his lap. "About as well as can be expected. I won't pretend that I'm not deeply wounded by Ernie's death. If he'd merely suffered a heart attack or stroke, I could bear it better." Sam saw Ernie's sightless eyes, the stab wounds in his stomach and the single slice across his neck again, saw the life-blood that had flowed and dried on Ernie's skin and clothes. "It's one thing to kill in war, terrible as that is, but to kill in cold blood." He shook his head.

"'Tis sometimes hard to contemplate how people can do such evil to each other," Lucy said.

Sam nodded. "True, but I shouldn't talk about this in front of ladies."

Her nostrils flared and Sam knew he was about to be chastised again. "Sam, I'm not some young girl afraid of any unpleasantness. I might be a woman, but I'm strong enough to deal with such things. Kindly remember that."

A smile played around his mouth as he inclined his head slightly. "Duly noted. You'll have to pardon my gentleman's upbringing."

An answering smile curved her lips. "You're forgiven. Now, what did yer examination reveal?"

"Not much, I'm afraid," he replied, raking a hand through his hair. "I didn't find a single clue on his body or clothes. The wounds were made with a common blade, there were no bruises from hands holding him down, either. Nothing to help Josh in his investigation."

The sympathy in her eyes warmed him. "Ye tried yer best. That's all any of us can do. I'm sure Josh will bring the culprit to justice."

Greta entered the parlor with a tray of tea and blueberry scones. "Listen to your intended, Sam. She's a wise young woman. You know Josh, he won't give up."

"Yes. You're both right, but let's change the subject if you don't mind." Sam took the cup of tea Greta held out to him. "I've had enough sadness for one day. Let's talk about happier things."

Lucy's heart went out to Sam. The deeper brackets around his mouth and the fatigue in his eyes showed the toll the situation was taking on him. It had been hard for her to see Ernie lying on the ground, bloody and broken, but it had to be infinitely worse for him. Determined to help him, she set out to cheer him up.

"Well, ye'll be happy to know that I'll be ready for our weddin' on Sunday. Greta is going to help me with any last-minute dress alterations," she said.

"That's very good news," Sam said. "I look forward to seeing you in it."

Greta chuckled. "She's going to be breathtaking, and no, you can't see it before the ceremony."

"I don't doubt she will be."

Lucy's cheeks heated as she caught Sam's appreciative gaze. She hid her shyness by taking a sip of tea. It was unsettling and exciting to have a man look at her that way. Men had looked at her with lust, but there was nothing nefarious in Sam's eyes.

"We'll need to ready the house for Lucy."

"What do you mean?" Lucy sat her cup on a stand next to her. "The house looked very ready when I visited yesterday."

Greta gave her an indulging smile. "Dear girl, a woman wants to make a house her own once she marries. You'll have your own ideas about decorating it, I'm sure. However, I'd like to offer my help, if you like."

Lucy saw the wisdom in accepting Greta's assistance.

Although she'd aided her mother in running their home, she had no idea what she wanted her own to be like. She'd been too busy helping to care for her younger siblings and performing endless chores to allow herself the freedom to dream about such things. But now…

"I'd be grateful for yer help," she said.

The mantel clock struck nine, startling them all.

"Goodness, I didn't realize it was so late," Lucy commented and began gathering up her sewing. "I should be on my way and get out of ya hair for the night, Greta."

"Nonsense, it was wonderful to have some company other than Darcy Wainwright's. She's a dear, but does go on about the most tedious things," Greta responded.

Sam stood up, a wry smile on his lips. "Yes, Mrs. Wainwright has a rather dry personality about her. I'll see you home, Lucy."

"I'd appreciate it," Lucy said.

After bidding Greta goodnight, they stepped out into the muggy night air. Sam offered Lucy his arm and she accepted it.

Glancing up at Sam, Lucy asked, "What drew you to this land, Sam? It seems an odd choice for a refined man such as yer self."

"Well, once the war was over, I was ready for a change."

Lucy frowned. "Yer said that once in your letters, but you didn't say much more than that."

His jaw tensed, and he looked up at the three-quarter moon overhead for a moment. "There's only so much of death and carnage a man can take, and I'd had more than my fill. Being a battlefield doctor is a grisly business and often my best efforts weren't good enough. I did my duty and was glad to serve my country, but once the war ended, I wanted to practice a different kind of medicine."

"I can understand that, but I'm sure there were plenty of hospitals to work for, or perhaps open your own practice in a city," Lucy inquired.

Sam chuckled softly. "You are a very determined woman, Lucy."

She smiled. "So I've been told."

Sam stopped, and Lucy halted beside him. "Have you ever wanted a completely different life? To do something new and challenge yerself?"

Lucy enjoyed his surprised expression when she laughed and took one of his hands. "Only every day since I was a lass of fourteen!"

Her pulse did a funny little leap when he kissed the back of her hand. "And tell me, fair Lucy, what are your dreams?"

Taken aback, Lucy could only stare at Sam. No one, not even her best friend back in Buffalo, had ever asked her what kind of future she wanted. Her parents were too busy supporting their large family to discuss their children's individual dreams. Lucy was so accustomed to keeping her desires to herself that it took her a few moments to find her voice.

"Ye'll laugh." She tried to pull her hand from Sam's, but he held onto it.

"I promise not to," he said.

Lucy drew herself up and met his eyes. "I've always been good at designin' clothing and would love to own my own boutique." She forced a laugh. "A silly dream, I know. Don't worry. I intend to honor our marriage and perform all my wifely duties to the utmost."

An odd look passed over Sam's face, and Lucy thought she'd angered him. "Lucy, I know you're probably used to the kind of men who expect you to be focused on seeing to a husband's needs before her own, but I'm not like those men. I want you to be happy, and if designing clothing makes you happy, so be it."

Once again, Sam had surprised her. She narrowed her eyes, suddenly suspicious. "Are you just testin' me?"

He squeezed her hands and smiled. "No, I mean it. I'm straightforward about my thoughts and feelings, and I don't believe in playing mind games. You'll always know where I stand."

Lucy relaxed, the tension leaving her shoulders. "I'm glad to hear that."

They resumed walking.

"We don't know exactly when little ones will come along," Sam said. "So, you'll have time to work on your designs and make clothes."

"Thank ya," Lucy said as they arrived at the Inn. "Both for walkin' me home and being so considerate."

They halted at the door.

"You're welcome. I have some patients to check on tomorrow morning, but how about we meet here for lunch?" Sam asked.

"I'd like that."

They fell silent, just gazing at each other for a couple of

moments. Then Sam leaned down and pressed a kiss to her cheek. Her breathing quickened at the feel of his warm lips on her skin.

When he pulled back, he said, "Goodnight, Lucy."

"Goodnight, Sam."

She gave him a brief smile and headed inside, chiding herself for being disappointed that he hadn't kissed her. There would be plenty of time for that, especially once they were married. Going to her room, Lucy readied for bed smiling with anticipation to see Sam the next day.

# CHAPTER 4

"*A*re you sure you don't mind?"

Lucy and Sam stood in his kitchen the next afternoon. They'd come out to his ranch so he could introduce her to his ranch hands, who hadn't been working near home the other day. However, they hadn't been there very long before a man had come galloping up to the house and announced that his teenage son had gotten stomped by a bull and needed help.

"Of course not, Sam," Lucy replied. "Go and don't worry about me. Do whatever you must to help the lad."

Sam smiled and kissed her hand. "All right. I'll be back as soon as I can."

Lucy nodded and watched him jog over to the barn, his medical bag in hand. She felt a rush of pride over finding such a kind, intelligent man. When Sam disappeared into the barn, Lucy turned her attention to the house. Taking a notepad, measuring tape, and a pencil from her purse, she started jotting down things she wanted for the house as she walked through it.

As she entered her room, she noticed movement when she looked out of the window that faced the driveway. Peering out of it, she saw someone standing at the end of the lane. She waited for them to approach the house, but they didn't. An uneasy feeling washed over her, and she stepped away from the window.

Going to Sam's room, she looked out the window. The figure was still there, only a little closer now. However, they were still too far away to tell if it was a woman or a man. Lucy was just about to go look out of a parlor window, when the lurker seemed to melt from sight.

She waited, but no one reappeared, either there or from anywhere outside the house. Putting her nervousness down to not being accustomed to being so alone, Lucy shrugged off her misgivings and went back to work.

AN HOUR LATER, Lucy was startled when someone knocked on the front door. She was in the pantry, taking stock of the supplies they were going to need. Hurrying to the door, she opened it, but no one stood on the other side of the threshold. She poked her head outside, but the porch was empty.

Stepping out onto the porch, Lucy scanned the yard and beyond, but didn't see anyone. The same feeling of dread flowed through her as before. Turning around, she stopped cold when she saw a small piece of paper fluttering in the breeze from a slightly raised nail in the wooden siding by the door. Swallowing her fear, she reached out and plucked the paper from the nail.

A note had been scrawled across it in pencil. *Get out while you can.* Lucy looked around again, her gaze stopping at every tree and scanning the buildings within her line of sight. Seeing nothing strange, Lucy went back in the house and locked the door.

She battled back fright as she closed and latched the windows and secured the kitchen door. It was another warm day, and it was going to get hot in the house. Better to be hot and alive instead of dead, though. She settled on a chair in the parlor where she could keep watch through a window. She looked at the note.

Its warning was clear, but why did someone want her to leave? She'd only been in Spruce Valley for two days. What kind of threat could she possibly be to anyone? So far, she'd only met six people and she certainly couldn't have offended them in such a short span. Could it have something to do with Ernie?

That didn't make sense since she'd never met the man. No, it must be some sort of cruel prank.

Her blood beginning to simmer, Lucy stood up, crushing the note and stuffing it in her dress pocket. She stomped to the kitchen door, fuming, not only at the person who'd written the note, but at her own cowardice.

Squaring her shoulders, she unlocked the door and yanked it open. A shadow fell across the threshold. Lucy stepped back, looked up, and screamed.

TURNING down the lane to his ranch, Sam was jerked from his thoughts by a woman's high-pitched scream. The sound sent a chill racing up his spine. Knowing the screams must be coming from Lucy, he spurred Atlas forward and the big equine lunged into a gallop.

Arriving at the house, Sam slowed his mount and slid from the horse's back before it had completely stopped. Running toward the house, he saw the kitchen door standing open, but he couldn't see inside.

"Lucy? Lucy!" he shouted, mounting the porch.

"Sam!" she screamed. "Stay back! He'll kill you!"

"Listen, my dear, I've told you that I'm Sam's frie—"

"Liar!" Lucy cried as Sam burst into the kitchen. "You wrote this dastardly note, and now ye've come to kill me!"

Sam's heart thudded against his ribs and then started to slow as he recognized both the cultured male voice and man standing in the middle of his kitchen.

"Lucy, he's telling you the truth," Sam said. "He's not here to kill anyone."

He hated the fear and anger in Lucy's wide-eyed, silver gaze. Her cheeks were crimson from the force of her emotions. She bravely wiped away a tear with one hand and

THE RECKLESS DOCTOR'S BRIDE

brandished a large knife in the other. She looked like a beautiful, sooty-haired goddess, bent on protecting others and meting out justice.

Her gaze moved from the would-be assailant to Sam. "He's not? Are you sure? Because I know a snake when I see one, and this man is a snake indeed."

Sam caught the twinkle in the man's midnight eyes but hid his own amusement in the face of Lucy's terror. "Lucy, I promise that he's my friend and he won't hurt either of us. You can put the knife down."

Lucy's gaze flicked back and forth between the two men. Slowly, she placed the knife on the counter but never took her eyes off the man.

Sam moved over to stand beside Lucy and put an arm around her shoulders. "Lucy, let me introduce you to Gray Jenkins. He's my foreman and a close friend. He lives in the bunkhouse along with two of my other hands. Gray, this is my intended, Miss Lucy Magee."

Gray swept off his gray cowboy hat and executed a deep bow to her. "It's a great pleasure to make the acquaintance of such a beautiful and brave woman such as yourself, Miss Magee."

Lucy glanced up at Sam and he gave her an encouraging smile. Then she stepped away from Sam and held out a hand to Gray. "Pleased to meet ya, sir. I'm sorry for threatening ya with a knife, but you frightened me when you just strolled in here and approached me the way you did."

Gray took her hand and gave it a gentle shake. "That's

quite all right. I'm not unaccustomed to being threatened, but I must say you're the most beautiful attacker I've ever met."

LOOKING in Gray's onyx eyes, Lucy's fear dissipated at the sparkle of humor in them. His handsome, angular features and the dimple in his left cheek were quite arresting and Lucy doubted that Gray ever lacked for female company.

"I see yer a flatterer," she teased. "I guess I'll have to keep my eye on yer."

Gray chuckled and released her hand. "Perhaps. Sam will have to make sure you're kept satisfied so I don't have a chance to swoop in and steal you away."

"Don't worry," Sam said smiling. "I intend to keep Lucy satisfied in every way."

Lucy's cheeks pinkened as his gaze roamed over her quickly before returning to her eyes.

"I'm sure you will," Gray remarked. "Well, I can give you my report later. I'll go settle in and find the others. See you tonight?"

Sam nodded. "I'll find you when I get home."

"Very good." Gray touched the brim of his hat. "Miss Lucy. It's been a pleasure to meet you, and I look forward to getting to know you. Good day to you."

"Good day, Gray." Lucy watched him walk out the door, his dark brown duster fluttering behind him. "He's quite the character," she said once he was out of earshot.

"Yes, he is. I've been friends with him since the moment

we met," Sam said. "He's one of those people you instantly like."

Lucy arched an eyebrow. "I might've if he hadn't scared the bejesus out of me. He waltzed in here like he owned the place and I thought he was the one who wrote this note."

She took the crumpled piece of paper from her skirt pocket and handed it to Sam. His jaw clenched as he read it and his eyes darkened with anger.

He turned the paper over and then back around. "There's nothing distinguishing about this paper. Did you see the culprit?"

Lucy hugged her middle. "I'm not sure. I was looking around and saw someone standing down at the end of the drive. It looked like a man, but I couldn't make out any features. Then they were gone, and I thought they went on their way.

"After a bit, there was a knock on the front door, but no one was there when I answered it. That's when I found the note. Then Gray showed up. I thought he'd left the note and meant me harm."

Sam moved closer and put his hands on her shoulders. "I'm sorry that you were frightened. I won't let anything happen to you, Lucy."

Sam's presence was comforting, and Lucy's fear abated somewhat as she looked into Sam's eyes. She believed that he would fight to keep her safe, but what happened when he wasn't around? Their ranch was as remote as many of the others, and if the ranch hands weren't nearby, she'd be vulnerable to anyone who meant her harm.

However, she didn't want to appear weak, so she didn't voice her fears. "I know. I'm sure it's just a prank of some sort." She forced a smile, hoping it looked genuine. "Most likely some youngster who thought it would be funny to scare a newcomer."

The right corner of Sam's mouth lifted. "That's possible. There are some scalawags around here, but I think it would be a good idea to teach you how to shoot a shotgun and pistol."

Lucy's pulse leaped at the thought. "Do you really think that's necessary?"

Sam nodded. "Yes. If no one else is around and a coyote or other predator shows up, you'll have to protect the livestock. We'll have a short lesson with the shotgun this afternoon."

Her palms grew damp at the thought of holding a dangerous weapon, but she saw the sense in Sam's words. "All right. But first, I'll make us a nice lunch with the things I brought with me."

Sam's eyes twinkled as he smiled. "I'm finally going to get to see what was in that big basket, hmm?"

Lucy turned away from him, giving him a coquettish smile over her shoulder as she moved to the counter on which the large wicker basket sat. "Aye. Why don't you go tend to something and I'll call you when it's ready?"

Sam's warm chuckle erased her lingering fear. "All right. I have something I can occupy myself with while you do that."

"Good. Off with ye then."

Lucy watched with amusement as Sam just shook his head and left the kitchen.

SITTING at his small desk in his bedroom, Sam looked out the window as he mused about what had happened to Lucy. Although he'd tried to reassure her that she was safe, he was more concerned than he'd let on. Was Ernie's murder connected with the warning note left for Lucy, or was someone else responsible? Either way, why would they threaten her?

Sam put down his pen and drummed his fingers on the desk as he considered how he was going to keep Lucy safe. He couldn't be with her all the time. He had patients to see and work around the ranch, too.

Pulling out his accounting ledger, Sam went over his budget. If he was careful with his funds, he could afford to hire someone to guard the ranch when he had to be away. The more he thought about it, the more Sam liked the idea. It would give them both piece of mind and they would only need a guard until Josh caught the murderer.

Lucy called him for lunch, and he smiled at the sound of her pretty, musical voice. He let her know he was on his way, straightened his desk, and went to join his future bride.

LUCY PUT her fork down and stared across the round table at Sam. "You want to hire someone to guard me?" The last bite of her lemon pound cake stuck in her throat a little as anxiety tightened her stomach. "Do you really think that's necessary?"

49

He wiped his mouth with a linen napkin. "Probably not, but I'm not going to take any chances. Like they say, better safe than sorry."

"Who will you hire?" Lucy took a sip of tea, hoping it would calm her.

Leaning back in his chair, Sam replied, "I'm not sure. I don't have any experience hiring guards, but I'm sure Josh can recommend someone."

To cover her disquiet, Lucy rose from the table and started gathering their dishes. "I'm sure he can."

She took them over to the sink and placed them in a pan of hot water. After adding some cold to it, Lucy wet a cloth and turned back to the table, intending to wipe it off. Sam pushed her back from it and stood up.

Her heart beat a little faster as he approached her with a half-smile. "Lucy, I'll make sure you're safe, so you can stop worrying."

"I'm not worried."

His smile broadened, stirring her ire.

"I'm not," she insisted, arching a haughty eyebrow.

Sobering, Sam said, "Lucy, you came here to marry me and even though we're not married yet, your welfare is my responsibility. I take my responsibilities very seriously, so when I say that I'll keep you safe, you can have complete confidence that I will."

The earnestness in his eyes bolstered Lucy's sense of security. "I believe ya and the idea of a guard does make me feel better."

Sam's smile returned, mesmerizing her with the way it

enhanced his rugged features. "Good. Now, I'll help you clean up and then start teaching you how to shoot."

Even though thinking about shooting again made her nervous, Lucy admitted that it also excited her. As they worked in companionable silence, Lucy both looked forward to, and dreaded, the coming lesson.

# CHAPTER 5

*T*he light of pride in Lucy's silvery eyes and the pretty pink flush in her cheeks sent desire flowing through Sam. Both of them had been surprised at how well Lucy had shot and that she'd enjoyed it so much.

"Just a few more shots," Lucy pleaded, as the breeze toyed with her ebony hair that had come loose from her long braid.

Sam grinned at her enthusiasm. "Not right now. We have to save some ammunition."

"All right," she agreed with a dejected expression. "I'm sure bullets are expensive, and we don't want to run out."

The flicker of fear in her eyes made Sam sober. "Right." He took the shotgun from Lucy and cradled it in the crook of his right arm. Putting his left arm around her shoulders, he guided Lucy toward the house. "You did very well for your first time. You'll be a crack shot before long."

Their close proximity enabled him to catch Lucy's scent.

She smelled like sunshine and lavender and he found the scent more intoxicating than the expensive perfumes some women wore.

"Thank ya. It was fun. I'm not afraid of guns now," Lucy responded. "I appreciate ye teaching me."

Her shoulder against his side felt nice and Sam was glad that she didn't object to his affectionate gesture. He gave her a gentle squeeze and then allowed his arm to fall away so she didn't become uncomfortable. "It was my pleasure. Is there anything else you need to do here?"

Lucy met his gaze. "No. I'm finished with my list."

Sam chuckled. "I'm sure it's a long one. I know this place needs a feminine touch."

Her smile drew his eyes to her lips. "Not very long."

"Well, get whatever you can from the mercantile and put it on my account. They also have catalogues there to order from," Sam said.

Lucy nodded. "All right. I'm a frugal person, so you don't have to worry about me spending all your money."

"I appreciate that," Sam said. "But I want you to have the things you'd like. I want to make you happy."

As they mounted the porch steps, Lucy said, "I'm here with a handsome man who just showed me a very nice afternoon and it's a beautiful sunny day. I'm already happy, Sam."

He gave a short laugh, pleased by her compliment. "So, you think I'm handsome, do you?"

She sent him a bright smile. "Ye know you're handsome, Sam. I'm sure you've had plenty of women tell you that."

"A few have mentioned that," Sam teased, moving closer. "I'm glad I meet with your approval."

Her eyes widened as he cupped her cheek. "Ye certainly do."

Brushing his thumb over her cheek, Sam said, "Good. And you're the loveliest woman I've seen in a long time, Lucy." He slid an arm around her waist, pulling her lightly against him. "May I kiss you?"

Lucy's heartbeat leapt in her chest as Sam tightened his embrace. The feel of his hard torso against her body created an unfamiliar heat inside that had nothing to do with the warm day. His expression had sobered, and his eyes reflected desire.

She placed her hands on Sam's chest and enjoyed the firm muscles under her palms. Her eyes settled on his sensual lips and her pulse rose as the urge to kiss him overtook her.

"Yes, you may kiss me."

Sam lowered his head toward her, and Lucy's eyes fluttered shut as he brushed his mouth against hers. Her lips parted on a tiny gasp and she slid her arms around his neck. She felt Sam's hands splay over her back and gooseflesh broke out over her shoulders.

She followed his lead when he slanted his mouth over hers and deepened the kiss. Her senses were filled with Sam as he held her closer and intensified his kiss. Reason intruded in her mind as she remembered that they were standing outside in plain view.

With a gentle push on Sam's chest, Lucy broke the kiss, staring into his passion filled eyes. The hungry way he looked at her made her want to resume their kissing, but it wouldn't be proper for several different reasons.

"I'm sorry," Sam said, but he didn't seem very contrite. "I just couldn't help myself. You're so beautiful."

Lucy flushed at his praise but smiled. "It isn't that I didn't enjoy it, because I did. Very much. It's just that we're not married yet."

Sam tucked an errant lock of hair behind her ear. "Just because we're not married doesn't mean we can't do some sparking."

Lucy's brow puckered in confusion. "Sparking?"

"That's what the people around here call kissing and hugging," Sam said with a chuckle. "There's a line I won't cross, but I won't hide the fact that I'm attracted to you."

His nearness strongly affected Lucy, which was disconcerting. One part of her wanted him to take her back in his arms and the shyer part of her urged her to step back. "I'm glad ye are, and I'm attracted to ye, too."

He seemed to read her uncertainty. With a nod, he moved away. "That certainly bodes well for a marriage since I'd like children."

His statement shouldn't have embarrassed her but thinking about the act of child-making sent heat surging into her cheeks. "Aye," was all she could manage as Sam opened the kitchen door and held it for her.

As Lucy passed him and entered the kitchen, she kept her eyes averted. She started gathering up the things she wanted to take back to the Inn with her to hide her discomfort. However, at one point, she glanced up to find Sam looking at her with an amused gleam in his eyes. Ignoring it, she continued her work and was soon ready to leave.

"WHAT A DAMN SHAME. I hope Josh catches the miscreant soon," Gray commented as they sat in Sam's parlor that evening.

"I'm sure he will, but I just don't understand who'd want him dead. I'm glad Drake agreed to take over as my shepherd until I find a replacement."

Ernie's eldest son was a serious, taciturn young man, but he possessed keen intelligence and a kind heart.

Gray grunted. "Yes, he's a good lad. Why doesn't he want to take the job permanently?"

Sam smiled at the picture Gray made. He sat in a royal blue wingback chair in a pair of worn black trousers, white shirt, and a worn gray cowboy hat balanced on his crossed legs. He leisurely puffed on a black pipe and smoke wound toward the ceiling in lazy wisps. Gray was an odd pairing of sophisticated gentleman and ranch hand.

"Drake plans to leave for California in August and is saving up some money before he goes. He's going to join a friend out there to look for a gold claim," Sam replied.

"It's best they're not waiting long, then. I've heard that some veins are drying up."

Sam turned around, stretched his long legs out on the sofa

and rested his head on the arm. "He also wants to start out before the snow flies."

"That's smart, as is your choice in a bride."

Sam grinned over at Gray. "I wondered when we'd get around to that."

"She's feisty, beautiful, and intelligent. She'll do well out here once she gets used to things," Gray commented. "She's been a city dweller, so it might take her a little time to adjust. Plus, I doubt she's done much farming."

A wry smile curved Sam's mouth. "Which was something we discussed in our correspondence. She's used to hard work and I warned her that life here can be harsh and crude. I was completely forthcoming about there being no fancy city trappings and not much society life outside of church events. I made it clear that it might be a little lonely here, but she said it would be a nice change from living in an overcrowded apartment where she had to share a bed with one of her sisters."

Gray's eyes lit with humor. "And now she'll share a bed with you, which shouldn't be a hardship."

Sam laughed at his comment. "No, it won't, but I've agreed not to rush her. I hardly think she'll be ready for intimacy so soon."

Gray uncrossed and re-crossed his legs. "Some men aren't so considerate, but it doesn't surprise me that you are. Your decency is one of the reasons I like you."

"That's ironic coming from a reprobate like you."

"We balance each other out, Sam. You're the good guy everyone likes, and I'm the bad guy everyone likes," Gray quipped.

Sam's mood soured as he thought that he wasn't always a good guy. Shrugging off the negativity that tried to worm its way under his skin, he said, "I know the ladies certainly like your dark charms."

"Mmm. That and it seems as though American women have a fondness for foreign accents," Gray responded. "I confess to using mine to my advantage."

Sam said, "I agree that we Americans do like hearing a foreign tongue. Lucy's brogue falls nicely on the ear."

"That it does," Gray agreed, taking a last puff on his pipe. He knocked out the ashes into the ashtray on the coffee table and stood. "Well, tomorrow comes early, and I don't want my boss to get put-out with me for starting late, so I'll bid you goodnight."

Sam chuckled at his teasing remark. "Goodnight, Gray."

He watched his friend leave the room and heard the kitchen door shut. Although he was tired, he didn't feel sleepy. Rising, he went to the kitchen, locked the door, and poured a finger of whiskey into a glass. He took it to his room and sat down at his desk.

Picking up a tablet on which he'd been writing a medical article he was going to submit to a journal, he did some editing and added more to it. However, even while he worked, Lucy kept popping into Sam's mind.

When he'd started searching for a bride, he hadn't planned on finding a woman like her. He'd hoped to connect with a pleasant woman with whom he could have some stimulating conversation, but Lucy was so much more than that.

As he finished his article and started getting around for

bed, Sam smiled as he recalled the brave way Lucy had faced-off with Gray that afternoon. So much backbone! Sam knew that she wouldn't be a pushover and would keep him on his toes, but he looked forward to it. His last thought before sleep claimed him was that being married to Lucy would never be boring.

LUCY'S HEART lurched as her eyes snapped open but was unsure what had woken her. She'd fallen asleep sitting up in the overstuffed chair by her bed. The book she'd been reading slipped off her lap and the sound of it hitting the wooden floor startled her again.

A noise outside her door made her turn her head sharply to the left. Was someone in the hallway? As far as she knew, she was the only guest at the Inn, but perhaps someone had come in after she'd gone to bed. She waited, but the sound didn't come again.

Thinking she'd imagined it, Lucy stood and was just about to relight the candle by her chair when the unmistakable sound of a footstep in the hallway froze her in place. A furtive noise at the door caused her pulse to rise. Quiet footsteps faded from outside her door and then all was silent again.

Fighting to keep her fingers from shaking, Lucy lit a match and held it to the candlewick. As a flame grew, illuminating the room in dim light, she gathered her courage and moved toward the door. On the floor just inside the room lay a small piece of paper.

Lucy's breathing grew shallow as she bent down and picked it up. Taking it closer to the candle, she turned the paper over and read, "The longer you stay, the more danger you're in. Leave!"

Shock turned Lucy's legs weak and she returned to her chair before she fell over. She stared at the note for several moments before looking at the door. Although there was a strong lock on it, Lucy felt far from safe.

Should she go downstairs to Bill's apartment, off the kitchen, and alert him? Or make a run for Josh's house next to the jail? Fighting back tears of fear, Lucy decided against leaving her room. That would make her vulnerable since she didn't know her enemy's identity and she didn't have a weapon.

She wished she had one of Sam's pistols. The only weapon she had was her large sewing scissors. After retrieving them from her sewing bag, she lit a second candle and settled back in the chair to keep watch. Thinking about Sam helped calm her a little and occupied her mind with something pleasant. Despite growing drowsy, she spent most of the night dozing fitfully before dropping off into a deep slumber near morning.

"Lucy? Are you up? It's Sam."

Being woken by the now familiar, friendly voice of her future husband was a far more pleasant experience than the one Lucy had had last night. She stood quickly and laid her scissors on the lampstand beside the chair.

"Oh, um, one moment, Sam," she called to him.

Rushing to the mirror, she looked at her hair, relieved that it wasn't too messy. She re-braided it, washed her face and hands, and straightened her dress.

Once presentable, she pulled the door open and smiled up at Sam. His bulk filled the doorway and she felt safe now that he was there. Although she would've liked to hug him, she refrained.

"Good morning," he said. "You slept rather late. Are you feeling well?"

The way his eyes roamed over her was the gaze of a physician assessing a patient and the frown that formed on his mouth said he wasn't happy with what he'd found. "You have dark spots under your eyes."

Not prone to lying, Lucy couldn't bring herself to tell Sam a falsehood. "I'm sure I do. I didn't sleep much."

"Why not? Is something wrong?" he asked, concern deepening his frown.

Lucy tried to see past Sam into the hallway but couldn't. "I know this isn't proper, but we're going to be married soon, so what does it matter?" Stress and fatigue turned her tone sharper than she'd intended.

"What's not proper?"

"Please come in and shut the door," she replied. "I must show ye something."

Sam arched an inquisitive eyebrow, but he did as she'd asked.

Lucy retrieved the note from the lampstand and held it out to Sam.

NOTING the way Lucy's features tightened with anxiety, Sam's scalp prickled in warning as he took the paper from her. His eyes lingered on her for a moment before dropping to the note in his hand. Fury surged through him as he finished reading it, and he crushed it in his fist.

"Tell me exactly what happened," he requested, forcing himself to stay as calm as possible.

The sheen of tears in Lucy's eyes turned Sam's anger white-hot and he almost turned and punched a wall. However, she was scared enough already, and that kind of behavior wouldn't do either of them any good. Sam concentrated on keeping his anger at bay as he listened to Lucy recount the events of the previous evening.

When she finished, he said, "I'm so sorry, Lucy. I never imagined anything like this would happen when you came here."

She came closer and looked up at him with compassion in her eyes. "I know, Sam. It's not yer fault. Do you think this has something to do with Ernie?"

He blew out a frustrated breath. "I don't know, but I can't rule it out. We need to get married right away. I don't want you here one more night by yourself."

The way Lucy's eyes bulged out almost made him smile. "What? The wedding's not until Sunday. You said the preacher wouldn't be here until then."

Sam did smile then. "I know, but Paul and his wife got back sooner than they'd expected, so he can perform the ceremony now." He reached out to trail the backs of his knuckles down her soft cheek. "I couldn't bear it if something happened to you, Lucy. I need to know that you're safe, but I can't do that if you're not with me."

Lucy bit her bottom lip and Sam wanted to kiss her, to savor her taste and make them both forget about Ernie's death and threatening notes.

"I don't know." She took a step away from him. "I know the ceremony isn't going to be lavish, but to be in such a rush..."

"I understand," Sam said. "I wish with all my heart that it didn't have to be this way, Lucy, but you can't move in with me until we're married."

"Aye, I know." She shook her head. "It isn't that I don't want to marry ye, Sam. Don't think that. But a woman likes at least a little romance about such an important affair."

Sam gave her a sheepish smile. "And believe it or not, so do some men, myself included." After thinking a moment, he said, "I know! I'll hire whoever Josh recommends as a guard and they can stay in one of the other rooms here to make sure you're safe until Sunday. That way we won't have to rush, and we'll have some peace of mind. What do you think?"

Her bright smile made Sam glad that he'd suggested it.

"I think that I'm lucky to be marrying such a smart man."

He laughed. "I certainly try to be. Now, let's go downstairs so you can get some breakfast while I go talk to Josh. When I come back, I thought it would be nice to go out to the herd and have a picnic."

A frown flitted over her face before she put on a brave smile. "I would enjoy that.

Sam nodded. "Are you ready to go down?"

Lucy grabbed her drawstring purse from a wooden peg by the door. "Ready."

Sam would've offered his arm to her, but the hallway was narrow, so they had to walk in a single line. He led the way down to the dining room and seated her at a table. "I'll be back just as soon as possible. Enjoy your breakfast."

"I'll be here," Lucy quipped.

Sam chuckled. "You better be."

Lucy gave him a cheeky smile. "Don't be gettin' bossy, sir, or ye'll find yourself without a bride."

With a slight bow, Sam said, "I'll keep that in mind," and left Lucy to her meal.

# CHAPTER 6

*S*itting on a blanket in the shade of a tall maple tree that afternoon, Lucy couldn't remember the last time she'd felt so uncomfortable. Meeting Drake had been a strange experience. She'd never encountered anyone like him, and she wasn't sure what to say to him.

Her awkwardness around him had nothing to do with his mixed heritage. Rather, it was his quiet, reserved personality that unnerved her. Except when spoken to, Drake didn't engage in conversation. The scornful glances he shot Lucy's way did nothing to reduce her disquiet.

Once Sam had concluded his business with the shepherd, they'd retired to the cool spot and prepared their picnic lunch. With her belly filled with the delicious food Bill had prepared for them, Lucy relaxed against the maple tree and watched Drake and his dog, Scruffy, separate a few sheep from the rest of the flock.

Drake let out a short whistle and Scruffy circled the small group of sheep they'd been gathering.

"Tis Drake always so austere?" Lucy asked.

A small smile curved across Sam's lips. "Most of the time. But it's worse right now. Drake tends to withdraw even further when he's upset. He knows I'm always supportive, but it's rare that he seeks me out."

Sympathy rose in Lucy, and she felt bad for thinking such critical thoughts about the young man. "My da and I aren't close, but I'd still be sad if we lost him. Even though I'm far from home, I still feel a connection to him."

"I understand that. You might think I'm odd, but I do believe that our souls are connected to those of our loved ones. I think we can still feel each other even if we're separated by many miles," Sam responded. He took her hand. "I'm sure that we'll grow to be close like that over time."

His touch sent her pulse skipping. "I hope so."

Approaching hoofbeats interrupted them. A man rode up to their picnic area and pulled his horse to a stop. He dismounted and joined them under the tree. The sober expression on his handsome face told Lucy that something serious had happened.

Sam rose to his feet. "Hello, Mason. This is Miss Lucy Magee." He helped her stand up. "Lucy, Mason Crawford."

Mason smiled as he shook hands with Lucy. "Pleasure to meet you, ma'am."

"Likewise," Lucy responded.

"What brings you?" Sam asked.

Once again, a frown settled on Mason's face. "I wish my

visit was about something pleasant, but I'm afraid I'm bringing you bad news."

Sam's left eyebrow arched. "Oh?"

Mason glanced at the flock of sheep. "One of our hands found three dead ewes this morning. Their throats were cut, and they were just left there."

Lucy's eyes widened. "Why would someone do such a thing?"

"I don't know," Mason responded. "But I thought with what happened to Ernie, I'd better warn you. I don't know if it's related or not. I already told Josh about it."

"I'm sorry to hear of your trouble," Sam said. "I hope the culprit is caught. It might have something to do with Ernie, but to what purpose? I can't understand what anyone would have against him. As far as I know, he's never been involved with any shady characters."

Mason shook his head. "You'd know better than me. I didn't know him all that well. Just in passing."

"My father kept to himself a lot."

They all jumped a little. They hadn't noticed that Drake had joined them.

His dark eyes glittered with anger. "Many of us do because most people aren't kind to us."

Sam hated that he was right. The Red Dog family and the others in their village several miles west of Spruce Valley were tolerated by some, befriended by a few people, or treated with disdain and hate by the rest. Sam couldn't blame Drake for being bitter.

Mason's expression turned sheepish. "I'm sorry about that

Drake. I hope you know that Sam and my family are your friends."

Drake nodded once. "Yes. You were always good to my father, Sam. He thought well of you. Thank you for your kindness to him and our village."

Sam gestured at the flock of sheep. "If it wasn't for him, I wouldn't have this ranch, or a successful operation. He's the one who got me started and took such great care of the sheep. That's why I made him my partner." He gave Drake a speculative look. "I know you're planning on going to California, so I suppose I can't tempt you to stay by offering you the same deal as Ernie and I had?"

One of Drake's dark eyebrows lifted. "Have you thought about this? Are you sure?"

"I'm positive. Outside of Ernie, you're the best man for the job," Sam said. "You already know the herd, the routine, and you're knowledgeable about sheep care. You're dependable and work hard. So, the partnership is yours if you want it."

"I'll think about it," Drake said.

Sam smiled. "That's all I ask."

Mason turned to Drake. "Be careful out here. It might be a good idea to have someone else stay with you. You can take turns keeping watch."

Sam thought it was a good idea. "I agree. I'd be happy to pay a second shepherd. Do you know anyone who would be suitable, Drake?"

"My brother is a good shepherd and has a good dog, too," Drake replied.

"The job is his if he wants it," Sam said.

A small smile tugged at Drake's mouth. "I will not give him a choice."

Sam chuckled. "Something tells me that Robert doesn't dare argue with big brother."

"It's is true," Drake agreed.

He gave them all a curt nod and returned to the flock.

Lucy watched him go with a mixture of curiosity and relief. The man made her uneasy, but she wanted to know more about him. She decided to ask Sam more about Drake sometime.

"Well, I best get back home," Mason said. "It's been a pleasure meeting you, Miss Magee. You'll have to come to visit us and meet the family. They're all curious about you. Jenny, my wife, is the schoolteacher. Sam says you're an educated woman. Jenny would enjoy visiting with another book-smart lady. Come over anytime."

Lucy beamed at him. "I would like that very much. Thank yer."

Mason touched the brim of his hat. "You're welcome."

He mounted his horse and headed back the way he'd come.

"He's very nice," Lucy commented.

"Yes, he is," Sam said. "His family are good people. His parents and aunt and uncle are the original settlers of Spruce Valley. This whole valley and the mountains in the distance are full of spruce trees."

"That makes sense," Lucy said as she repacked their picnic basket.

Once they finished cleaning up, Sam stowed their things in the buggy and helped Lucy into it. He climbed in and sat looking at the flock of sheep that grazed on the rich, green grass.

"'Tis peaceful" Lucy remarked.

Sam nodded. "Yes. I just hope it stays that way now."

So did Lucy, but as they drove back to Sam's ranch, a shiver of trepidation ran through her. She suspected the killer wasn't done causing trouble for the citizens of Spruce Valley.

Sitting in the sheriff's office later that afternoon, Sam told Josh about Lucy's nocturnal visitor and gave him the wadded-up note.

Josh unfolded it and smoothed it out on his desk, which was just an old wooden table. A couple of dime store novels were stuck under one leg to keep it level and scars crisscrossed its worn surface. Concern was etched on his face as he got up and went to a large wooden crate that sat on a table by one of the two windows in the front part of the building.

With amusement, Sam watched Josh rummage around in the crate, pulling out file folders until he found the one that he wanted. Unlike his own tidy filing system, the sheriff's disorganized method of records keeping confused Sam. It amazed him that Josh knew where anything was. His house was much the same way, with stacks of newspapers and books lying all over the place.

Josh took out another small piece of paper from a file and

came back to his desk. Sam recognized the first note that someone had left at the ranch and his temper started to rise.

Laying the notes side-by-side, Josh examined them. "The writing matches. The letters are formed the same way."

Sam rose and joined Josh, looking over his shoulder at the notes. "You're right. Both are printed, not written in cursive."

Josh rubbed his chin. "Could be that whoever wrote them isn't all that educated. Everything is spelled right, but the printing is kinda crude."

Sam nodded. "Which should help us narrow down the suspect list."

Josh grinned up at him. "Us? Are you fixing to be a deputy?"

"No, no." Sam held up a hand in protest. "I'm perfectly happy being a doctor and rancher. I don't need a third occupation."

"Too bad. I could use one," Josh commented. "Anyway, I'm going over to the station to look at Damon's records. People are always signing IOU's and such. I might find a handwriting match."

"That's a great idea," Sam said. "I didn't think about that."

"That's why I'm the sheriff and you ain't," Josh teased. "Now, get out of here so I can go do my job."

"DON'T BE NERVOUS," Greta said.

Lucy tried to relax as she sat beside Greta on the seat of her buggy. Greta's gelding, Topper, stood patiently waiting for instructions. Seeing that her knuckles had turned white from the force with which she held the reins, she loosened her grip.

"I'm sorry. It's just that I've never driven or ridden a horse before," she said. "Back home, we walked everywhere unless we had a few extra coins to spare on a cab. That was rare, though."

Greta nodded. "I understand, but as you can see, things are far away from each other here. Walking would take forever, and it's just not practical."

Lucy knew that Greta was right. "I see what ye mean."

Greta cleared her throat. "Also, it's not a good idea to walk for long distances alone. Sometimes unsavory characters come through the area, and they may be lonely for the company of a woman. They may avail themselves of the opportunity to take advantage of a woman out by herself."

A chill ran through Lucy as she thought about the day she'd arrived in Spruce Valley. She'd walked at least a couple of miles by herself in the pouring rain. Lucy tried not to think about what might have happened if a disreputable character had happened upon her before Sam and Josh had arrived. She saw the wisdom in Greta's statement. Determined to be as self-sufficient as possible, Lucy straightened her spine and took up the reins in a more confident manner.

"All right, then. I'm ready for my lesson," she said. "I refuse to be a victim, and I don't want Sam to worry about me when he can't be around."

Greta patted her shoulder. 'Atta girl. We'll make an expert driver out of you in no time."

Lucy smiled. "I don't know about that, but I want to be as good a driver as possible."

"Well then, let's get started, shall we?"

With an emphatic nod, Lucy said, "Let's."

Greta began instructing Lucy, showing her how to talk to Topper as well as guide him with the reins. The gelding was responsive and didn't require a heavy hand. Greta had Lucy stay at a walk the whole way through town to allow her to become accustomed to the horse's movements, and to get the hang of maneuvering the horse to the right or the left.

As they left town, Greta smiled at Lucy. "You're doing very well, my dear. You seem to be a natural at this."

Lucy chuckled. "You're very kind to say so."

Greta responded with a small snort. "No, I only give credit or praise when it's truly due. Otherwise, how will one learn the proper way to do anything if their mistakes are praised? Besides, telling you that you're doing well when you really aren't is a lie, and I hate lying and deceit. I refuse to engage in such behavior."

The stern way Greta spoke piqued Lucy's curiosity, and she wondered what might have happened in Greta's past to make her so rigid concerning the subject. However, it was none of her business, so Lucy kept her questions to herself. Instead, she returned her attention to the task at hand.

"You're right," she said. "I can't learn properly that way. Thank you for your honesty and for taking the time to teach me."

"You're welcome," Greta said. "I'm sure Sam would've gotten around to it at some point, but I thought that I could start you off in the meantime. I believe that women should be as self-reliant as possible, and out here a woman must be able to get along without a man. This is especially true for ranchers' wives. There are times when they must be able to run the ranch while their husbands are away on cattle drives."

Lucy hadn't thought of that and she wondered if Sam ever went on cattle drives. If so, that meant that she would be in charge of the day-to-day operations of the ranch.

"Of course, you won't have to worry about that since Sam has a reliable foreman and good ranch hands. He doesn't like to leave his patients in the lurch, so he doesn't usually go along on the cattle drives."

"I won't lie, I'm relieved to hear it," Lucy said. "At least until I become more settled here, I would prefer to not be left alone like that."

Greta instructed Lucy on how to guide the horse around a sharp bend in the road before saying, "That's perfectly understandable, but I don't think you have to worry about that. Sam will never leave you alone with what's going on, so don't fret."

"I'm glad," Lucy said.

Their conversation turned to more pleasant things. They discussed Lucy's upcoming wedding and her worries disappeared as anticipation grew within her to marry her handsome doctor.

# CHAPTER 7

*L*ucy smiled to herself as she dressed for bed that evening. It had been a long day but very productive. Greta had taught her how to collect eggs from the chicken coop, how to milk cows, and how to unhitch and re-hitch a horse to a buggy.

Then they had made a list of pantry items that Lucy needed to stock up on, so that everything would be in place when the ranch became her home and she and Sam began their life together. Lucy took her responsibilities as a wife seriously, and she would make their home as nice as possible.

She was just about to change into her nightgown when someone knocked on her door. Fear made her heart lurch and she was leery about answering the door. However, it might be Sam stopping by for some reason, so she moved to the door and asked, "Who is it?"

"Hello, Miss Magee. My name is Grant Carlson, the man Sam sent to guard you."

Lucy was still cautious. "What's the code word?"

"Pink bow," came the reply.

A smile lit Lucy's face and she opened the door. A man of average height with light brown hair stood in the hallway. Although he was rather ordinary-looking, his dark blue eyes were filled with intelligence, and his bearing bespoke a man who was confident. There was an alertness and vitality about the man that assured Lucy that Mr. Carlson would keep her safe.

"How do you do?" she greeted him.

"Just fine, thanks for asking. And yourself, ma'am?"

"I'm very well, thank you. I appreciate you coming. I must confess that it does bring me comfort."

Grant smiled, which revealed a dimple in his right cheek and made him look more handsome. "I'm glad to hear it. That's the idea." He pointed to a chair that sat in the hallway. "I'll be right out here if you need anything."

Lucy frowned. "That chair doesn't look very comfortable."

"That's all right. It'll keep me awake," Grant replied.

"I have an extra pillow you could use to cushion the seat," Lucy suggested.

Grant shook his head a little. "I appreciate your kindness, ma'am, but I'll be fine."

"Are ya sure?"

"Yes."

Upon his assurance, Lucy bid him goodnight and shut the door. As she readied for bed, a feeling of peace came over her.

Knowing that Grant was guarding her gave her a sense of security, and when she laid down in bed, it wasn't long before she fell into a deep slumber.

SAM MOPPED sweat from his brow as he came out of Olivia Carstead's bedroom. Her midwife, Julia Simmons, had sent Olivia's husband Richard to fetch Sam when complications had arisen. The baby had been breach, and Julia hadn't been able to turn the infant to the proper position.

Since he was friendly with the Crow tribe, Sam had developed good relationship with a few of the midwives in the village. They were adept at turning babies, and he'd traded some quality material for lessons in their methods.

They attempted massage techniques first, only using internal manipulation as a last resort. Sam was relieved that he'd mainly been able to turn Olivia's baby with massage. He'd only had to manually turn the infant the last couple of inches to finish aligning it with the birth canal.

Once it was in place, the baby had slipped out with a minimum of effort on Olivia's part. It was a good thing, because she'd been weak from all the unproductive labor before he'd arrived.

He descended the stairs and entered the Carstead's parlor. Richard sat stone-faced on the couch and looked up when Sam walked into the room.

Sam gave him a reassuring smile. "You have a healthy little girl, Richard, and Olivia is doing just fine. She'll need to rest as much possible for a couple of days, but she'll recover quickly."

Richard stood up. Relief and joy spread across his features and his pallor improved. "A daughter. I'll bet she's as pretty as her ma. I sent for my sister. She said she'd come stay with us for a week or so once the baby came."

"Good," Sam said. "I'm sure she'll be a big help."

Richard held out a hand to Sam and they shook hands. "Thanks for everything, Sam. I can't tell you how much I appreciate you coming."

Sam smiled. "Well, that's what doctors are supposed to do."

Richard's gaze lowered and he shifted his stance nervously. "I don't get paid until Friday. The baby came a little early, so we didn't have the money put aside yet."

This didn't come as a surprise to Sam. Few people around Spruce Valley were of moderate means and rarely had enough money between checks to save any.

It was one of the reasons Sam had gone into a business that would keep his head above water. He wasn't going to get rich practicing medicine in the small town, but he hadn't moved there to make money.

"Friday is just fine, Richard. There's no rush. Just enjoy your little one."

"Thanks again," Richard said.

Sam nodded, clapped the man on the shoulder, and took his leave.

Putting Atlas into a brisk trot, Sam's mind turned to Lucy. He hoped she was having a good day. When he'd checked in with Grant, he'd been relieved to hear that all had been quiet overnight.

Grant had informed Sam that Lucy had gone out to the ranch with Greta to do some more work. It made Sam feel good that Lucy had such a keen interest in making their house homier. She was also so beautiful, and Sunday couldn't come soon enough for Sam. He wanted to hold her in his arms and show her how wonderful passion could be. Although he never asked her, Sam suspected that Lucy was a virgin based on the hesitant way she kissed him.

He would take his time on their wedding night so that he didn't scare her, and he would also give her as much pleasure as possible. The thought of making love with Lucy made his temperature rise a little, and Sam pulled his thoughts away from that. Instead he wondered what she was doing right then.

At dinner last night, her excitement over all she'd accomplished yesterday had amused him. Her account of her first time milking a cow had left him in stitches, and Sam was looking forward to many such conversations throughout the coming years. How wonderful it would be to have her presence in their house, hear her laughter, and hold her close every night…

A shot rang out, the unexpected sound making Sam jerk the rains and Atlas veered to the left. Sam pulled Atlas to a halt as anger turn his blood hot. He looked around for the inconsiderate shooter but saw no one.

"Who's there? Come out here!" he demanded.

Silence.

Sam's temper rose. "Fine. Stay hidden. But be more

considerate and refrain from shooting so close to riders on the trail."

A second shot was fired and this time the shot was so close that Sam could hear the bullet whiz past his head. Sam had seen enough combat to know when someone was shooting at someone on purpose. The events of the last few days came back to Sam. He knew that the shooter might very well be the person who had left the two notes for Lucy, and Ernie's murderer.

Sam didn't waste time trying to speak with the shooter. He put his heels to Atlas' sides and clicked to him. The big horse sprang into motion, snorting as he caught Sam's urgency.

Crouching low over Atlas's neck, Sam gave the stallion his head. Atlas's strides lengthened and they sped away. Two more shots were fired, but Sam didn't bother looking back. He urged Atlas to increase his pace and they flew down the road.

When no further shots were fired, Sam slowed Atlas to conserve his energy. He listened closely, but he heard no horse hooves behind him on the road, nor did he hear any noise coming from the woods that lined both sides of the road.

Had he outrun the culprit. Was there more than one? Could it be a team working together? It was possible, Sam supposed, but what was their motivation? He'd been sitting still, giving the shooter an easy shot. Unless the culprit was blind or a terrible shot, there was no way they couldn't have hit him. That meant that the responsible party had intended to miss.

Had someone with a sick sense of humor just been toying with him? It was possible, but Sam doubted it. After every-thing that had happened, Sam didn't believe that was the case.

However, he didn't waste time pondering it. Reaching safety was more important right now.

With that in mind, he alternated Atlas's gait between a canter and a trot. He was going to stop in town, which was on the way, so that he could tell Josh about the incident. Then he would head home to make sure that Lucy and Greta we're safe, even though he knew that Gray would be on the lookout for anything suspicious. As he made his way along, Sam prayed that no harm would befall anyone at home.

LUCY AND GRETA were in the parlor trying to decide what material to make curtains with. Since the walls were cream colored, almost any print would work. Lucy had bought three different kinds of cloth: a pretty blue, white and gold floral pattern, a solid heavy dream brocade, and a deep maroon with silver stripes.

"I can't make up my mind," Lucy said. "I don't want them to be too feminine. That would most likely make Sam uncomfortable." She stood back to consider again while Greta held up first the maroon material against the wall, and then the blue flowered cloth.

"I'm just not sure," she said.

"Well, you might have to ask Sam for his opinion in that case," Greta said.

"Yes, I think I will."

A horse trotted up to the house and Lucy looked out the window. Sam was dismounting Atlas and Lucy smiled at how handsome he looked. His blond hair was tousled and wind-blown and his shirt was rumpled, but he still made her heart beat faster.

He was virile and strong, and Lucy had never encountered a man like him before. She couldn't believe that some pretty woman hadn't snared him before now, but Lucy was glad that no one had. It was her good fortune to have found someone like him.

He wound Atlas's reins around the hitching post near the kitchen and walked toward the porch. The determined set to his jaw and his swift strides made Lucy concerned.

"Sam's home," she said. "He doesn't look happy. I hope nothing went wrong with Mrs. Carstead's delivery."

Greta echoed her sentiments as they went to the kitchen. Sam was just coming through the door when they entered the room.

His eyes roamed over both women. "Is everything all right?" he asked. "Has there been any trouble today?"

A prickle of fear raised goosebumps along Lucy's arms. "Nay, Sam. All is well. What's happened?"

He raked a hand through his hair, messing it up even more as he crossed the room to the two women. "There's no way around telling you. I had a nasty experience today."

His tense expression set Lucy's nerves even more on edge. "Are ye hurt?"

Sam shook his head. "No. I'm fine."

"Thank heavens," Greta said. "Now, tell us what happened."

Gathering his thoughts, Sam debated giving the women a gentler version of events, but downplaying the danger might put them in more jeopardy. Plus, Lucy and Greta weren't the kind of women who had to be protected from unpleasant subjects.

Opting to tell them the truth, he recounted his story. By the time he was finished, both women's eyes were huge with shock.

Lucy put a hand to her throat. "Who would do such a heinous thing? Why would anyone want to hurt you?" She inhaled a sharp breath. "Do you think it's the same person who's been leaving those notes?"

"What notes?" Greta asked.

Sam and Lucy exchanged a glance. He nodded in answer to Lucy's silent question, so she filled Greta in on the situation.

"Good heavens!" the older woman said. "It can't be a coincidence. The two things must be related."

"I agree," Lucy said.

Crossing the kitchen to a cabinet, Sam took out a small decanter of bourbon and a tumbler. "You'll have to pardon me, ladies, but I need just a touch to steady my nerves. It's not every day that someone shoots at me."

He poured a finger into the tumbler and took a sip before returning the decanter to its place.

Lucy went to him. "I'm not offended in the least, Sam. Who could blame you after being through something like that?"

Greta echoed her sentiments.

"Thank you both for being so understanding," Sam said with a tight smile.

"Of course," Lucy said.

Sam took another sip of his drink and then paused before he swallowed as a thought occurred to him. What if it hadn't been a prank? Could they have followed him home? He hadn't heard a horse behind him, but if the culprit knew him, they wouldn't have to give chase.

Fighting back panic, Sam downed the rest of his bourbon and set the tumbler on the counter. "I have to speak with Gray. I'll be back. Stay inside."

LUCY LOCKED the door behind Sam and turned to face Greta. Her own fear was reflected in her friend's eyes.

"I'm sure Sam will get to the bottom of it," Lucy said. "It'll be fine."

Greta gave a little nod. "I'm sure you're right. Now, let's do something to stay busy until Sam comes back. There's no sense letting time go to waste since there's a lot to be done."

"I think that's a fine idea," Lucy said, picking up a bolt of white eyelet material. "I think this will make very nice curtains for the kitchen. Do you?"

"Oh, yes. If we put some gathers in them, they'll look pretty…"

As the women went back to work, they tried to combat their anxiety over the situation but weren't completely successful. They knew it was serious, and no amount of work could keep their worry at bay.

While they measured material, Lucy prayed that Josh would figure out who was behind all of this. She also hoped that it would be accomplished by their wedding day, which was fast approaching.

*Please, Lord, don't let anything ruin our special day,* Lucy thought. *I want to look back and remember it as a time of joy, not fear. I pray that You will grant us at least that one day of peace.*

# CHAPTER 8

*I*t seemed as though Lucy's prayer had been answered. No further incidents occurred, and she hoped that all the unpleasantness was over.

One day while she was shopping in Frost's Mercantile, she met Jenny Crawford, Mason's wife. Lucy liked Jenny right away and invited her to have tea with her. They went to The Eatery, which was situated at the rear of the store.

Lucy found the feisty, intelligent redhead amusing. It was also nice to talk with a woman who was as educated as she.

Nell, the waitress at The Eatery, came over to their table, and Jenny introduced her to Lucy. They exchanged pleasantries. Lucy thought that although mildly attractive, Nell appeared to be a rather sober soul, almost listless, in fact.

Nell then proceeded to take their order, and Lucy thought that the process was rather odd.

"What do you recommend, Nell?" Jenny asked.

All at once, Nell's demeanor changed. Her face lit up and her eyes sparkled, and Lucy wondered if the woman who'd approached their table had been swapped out for an identical twin.

"Today we have a very nice shepherd's pie with a tasty, flaky crust. Emmet also made applesauce and Ella baked cherry and custard cream pie."

Jenny smiled. "Then I'll have the shepherd's pie and the cherry pie for dessert."

"You won't regret it," Nell assured her. "And for you Miss Magee?"

Lucy wondered at the hope in Nell's eyes and glanced at Jenny, noting the conspiratorial smile on her lips. "Um, well, I've had lunch already, and I don't think I could eat the shepherd's pie." She glanced at Jenny again, then back at Nell. "Perhaps ye could recommend something a bit lighter that would go well with a cup of tea?"

Nell's smile returned. "We have a dandy jelly cake that would be very nice with tea."

"That's what I'll have, then," Lucy said. "Thank you for your help."

"You're welcome, miss. I'll get your order in right away."

Lucy and Jenny traded smiles as Nell hurried off.

"Not many people realize it, but Nell has a keen mind," Jenny said. "Most people here order the same sort of thing when they come, which bores Nell. She needs more of a challenge, and she likes seeing the patrons enjoying something different."

"Oh, I see," Lucy responded. "I wasn't sure what to do at first, but I'm glad I followed your lead."

Jenny's eyes glittered with mischief as she whispered, "My husband calls me a witch because I can convince people to do things."

Lucy giggled. "Can ye cast spells?"

Jenny pressed a hand to her mouth to muffle her laughter and shook her head. "Perhaps. Beware, or I may cast a spell on you."

They laughed over their silliness but sobered when Nell returned with a large silver tray. She placed a very pretty porcelain teapot with a pink rose design on it and two matching teacups on the table. With a smile that was a trifle smug, Nell began fixing their tea.

The other women watched in fascination as Nell performed a proper tea-making ritual with flair and confidence. When she was done, she sat a perfect cup of tea in front of each of them.

Lucy took a sip of hers and looked at Nell. "This is lovely, Nell. It's clear that yer an experienced tea maker. No disrespect to the Inn, but this is the best cup of tea I've had since I came here."

Nell beamed at her. "Thank you for saying so. I'm glad you like it."

"That I do," Lucy said. "Where did you learn to make such fine tea?"

A mysterious smile curved Nell's mouth. "That's a story for another time. I have to get back to work. I'll be back with your food soon."

She was gone before they could respond.

"That's a little peculiar," Jenny remarked. "I wonder what else she's hiding, not that it's any of my business, of course."

"Nor mine," Lucy agreed. "Still, I can't help being curious. It's not just anyone who can make tea like this." She took a sip. "It's as good as my ma's and she was makin' it from the time she was a young lady."

Jenny also sampled hers. "Yes. I grew up around society ladies and worked as a governess for a wealthy family. This is as fine as any I've ever tasted."

Lucy refrained from commenting further because she didn't want Nell to overhear them discussing her. She also didn't want Jenny to think she was a busybody. "Well, perhaps one day, she'll tell us her story if we're patient."

Jenny murmured her agreement and changed the subject. "Your wedding day is almost here. Are you excited to be marrying the handsome Dr. Slater?"

Lucy's cheeks turned pink as she smiled. "Aye. I never imagined that I'd be marryin' such a good man. I can scarcely believe it."

"I understand what you mean. I'm fortunate to have found a man like Mason. He's kind, decent, and hard working."

Lucy grinned. "Not to mention pleasing to the eye."

Jenny laughed. "He certainly is. When I first saw him, I wouldn't have been surprised it he'd introduced himself as Adonis."

Nell returned with their orders, and the ladies continued conversing about Lucy's upcoming wedding as they ate their meal. Lucy thoroughly enjoyed her jelly cake, impressed by the moist, flavorful layers. The slight acidic taste of the raspberry jelly meshed well with the sweetness of the cake, which had a bit of a spicy bite to it.

By the time they were finished, Lucy's spirits were high, both from Jenny's entertaining company and the delicious fare. She and Jenny made plans for her and Mason to join Lucy and Sam for dinner at the Inn on Friday evening.

Jenny said, "Mason and Sam can amuse each other while we go over your wedding dress after dinner."

Lucy eagerly agreed. "Instead of going home in the dark, why don't you and Mason spend the night at the Inn?" she suggested.

Jenny smiled. "That's a great idea. Then I could help you dress for the wedding."

"Do you think Mason would mind?"

A gleam entered Jenny's eyes. "Don't worry. I have ways of convincing him."

Lucy chuckled. "I think he may be right about you using witchcraft."

They paid their bill and parted ways. Lucy walked to Sam's office. He was with a patient, so she stayed in the small lobby. With the natural pine walls and two windows, it was a nice space, but like their home, it was plain and needed some sprucing up.

Looking around, Lucy envisioned sheer curtains and pretty green drapes that could be drawn in the winter to help insulate the room. The small black pot-bellied stove wasn't in use right now but come fall, it would need to be kept going much of the time. Sam had explained to her that it wasn't unusual for them to have light snow and freezing temperatures by the middle of October, so a fire would be necessary.

The door to Sam's examination room and office area opened, and a young woman holding a baby exited it.

Sam followed them. "Just give him half a teaspoon of that medicine twice a day and his belly will be just fine, Mrs. Harrington."

"Thank you, Dr. Slater," Mrs. Harrington said.

"You're welcome." Sam spotted Lucy. "Allow me to introduce you to my betrothed."

The introductions were made, and the two women exchanged pleasantries.

Lucy said, "You have a beautiful baby boy."

Mrs. Harrington smiled down at the infant. "Thank you. He's eight months old now, and he's the apple of our eye."

"I can see why. He's darling."

Mrs. Harrington thanked her again and went on her way, leaving Sam and Lucy alone.

"All done with your shopping?" Sam asked.

Lucy lifted her large basket a little. "Yes. I found everything I need."

"Good. I'm afraid I have patients to see the rest of the day, but would you care to dine with me this evening at the Inn?" he asked.

Lucy lifted her chin. "Only if you allow me to pay. Ye've bought me several meals, and I feel that I should reciprocate."

Sam considered that for a moment. It went against his

upbringing for a woman to pay, but the stubborn set to Lucy's jaw made him realize that arguing with her would be futile. "Very well. Does six o'clock suit you?"

"That'll be just fine."

He moved closer and Lucy's pulse leapt. "May I have a taste to tide me over until then?"

Kissing Sam had been a heady experience and Lucy wanted to feel it again. She nodded as he cupped her face. His hands were warm and gentle as he tipped her chin up. Warmth spread through Lucy as he lowered his head and pressed his lips to hers.

It felt so natural to wind her arms around his neck and lean into Sam. Lucy's breathing quickened when he embraced her waist and slanted his mouth over hers, deepening the kiss. Lucy loved the way his hard torso felt against her body, and she could've gone on kissing him forever. But all too soon, Sam gentled the kiss and broke it.

She noted that his chest rose and fell rapidly as he rested his forehead against hers. "Do you have any idea what you do to me?"

His voice held a husky quality that sent a shiver through Lucy. "I think it's the same thing you do to me."

He smiled and kissed her cheek. "I was hoping we'd be attracted to each other, but I didn't expect it to be so strong. Is it just me?"

Lucy sighed as his lips grazed her earlobe. "No, Sam. It's not just you."

Sam kissed her cheek again and stepped back from her.

"I'm glad to hear it. I think it's best if you leave now while I can still resist kissing you again."

Lucy wanted him to take her back in his arms, but she knew he was right. "Aye. I'll see you this evening."

Sam gave her a slight bow. "This evening."

Lucy smiled at his gallant gesture and exited the office.

# CHAPTER 9

*I*t had rained during the night, but the day of Lucy's wedding began with bright sunlight and fresh air. She woke to the scent of coffee and bacon, but anxiety hit Lucy and, although it smelled delicious, her stomach rejected the idea of eating. Rising from her bed, Lucy went to the washstand, poured some water in the basin, and splashed her face with it.

She dried it with the towel hanging on a nearby peg and took several deep breaths. Although she'd been looking forward to marrying Sam, now that the day was here, doubt assailed her. What if she wasn't a good wife? What if Sam wasn't what he seemed?

Stories of disappointed brides were sometimes in the newspapers back home. As she went to the tiny closet in her room, she dismissed the idea that Sam would change once they were married. Too many people had told her that he was a fine man for it not to be true.

Someone knocked on her door.

"Just a moment," she responded, donning a robe on her way to answer it. "Who is it?"

"It's Jenny. I've brought you some tea."

Relief flooded Lucy and she rushed to open the door. "God bless you," she said, admitting Jenny inside.

Jenny smiled and set a small tray with a little teapot and two cups on the dresser. "I remember how I felt on my wedding day. I thought some tea would help settle your nerves."

"I'm grateful to you."

Lucy stirred a little sugar and cream into her tea and took a sip. The hot brew slid down her throat and started soothing her. She closed her eyes and sighed. Her eyes reopened when Jenny chuckled.

"You remind me of Mason when he drinks his first cup of coffee," she said.

Lucy smiled. "There's nothing so lovely as nice hot tea first thing in the morning."

"And what a lovely morning it is, too," Jenny remarked, going to the window. "Especially for a wedding."

Lucy took another sip to combat a little stab of anxiety. "Aye." She looked at Jenny. "Tell me, did ya ever doubt coming here to marry a man ya didn't know? Is Mason still the man you first married?"

Jenny sipped her tea and then shook her head. "No, he's not. He's even more wonderful than I thought he was when we first met. You have nothing to fear, Lucy. Sam is very respected here, and if I had any doubts as to his character, I'd tell you."

Her friend's words went a long way to allay Lucy's fears. "Thank you. I feel better about that now, but I still worry that I won't be a good wife. There's so much about ranching that I don't know."

Jenny smiled. "I also grew up in a city and I never did any sort of manual labor outside of a bit of cooking. Luckily, I had Cecilia to teach me, and I'm quite good at many things now. You will be, too. I'll teach you and so will Greta. You'll be proficient in no time."

"I hope so." Lucy took a deep breath. "Well, enough of that. I'd better start getting ready. I don't want to be late and I want to look my best."

"Don't worry. By the time we're done, you'll look like a princess."

Lucy laughed and started getting dressed.

"You look so handsome that you'll make her swoon."

Sam smiled at Gray's reflection in the mirror he stood before. "I don't know about that, but I do still fill out a suit nicely. It's been a long time since I wore one."

Gray turned him around and adjusted his tie a little. "Not much call to wear a full suit out here when you're gallivanting around the countryside to treat patients."

"You're right about that. I'd wear one out every week, and

I don't have the funds to constantly replace them," Sam agreed.

Stepping back, Gray raised an eyebrow. "You'd have more money if you stopped taking chickens and the like as payment."

Sam fixed him with an irritated look. "What am I supposed to do when people just don't have the money? I can't ignore their suffering, Gray."

"Yes, I know."

"I'll continue to build my practice, but I don't care about becoming rich. As long as the ranch brings in enough money to offset any financial loss my profession might cause, I'll be happy," Sam said.

"You must remember that you also have a bride to support now, Sam. She's relying on you to provide for her needs."

"I'm aware of that. I won't let us end up in the poor house," Sam responded. "Where is all this doubt coming from? I certainly don't need to hear it on my wedding day."

Gray's smile was tinged with remorse. "You're right. Forget I said anything." He consulted his pocket watch. "We should leave now."

Sam nodded and grinned. "I'm not the only one who looks dashing. You'll draw many female eyes today."

"I'm counting on it," Gray said, chuckling and smoothing down his black suit jacket.

Sam laughed and shook his head. "You'll never change. Come on. Let's go."

Gray followed Sam outside where his horse and buggy awaited them. As he climbed in and took up the lines, Sam sought to quell the uncertainty his conversation with Gray had created. He wasn't rich, but he could give Lucy a good life, couldn't he?

His mind turned toward his finances and his doubt faded as he thought about the money he had saved up. There was no bank in Spruce Valley and running to the one in Helena wasn't practical, so he had his money stashed under a floorboard in his room.

There was plenty there to take care of their immediate needs and pay his hands. Sam shrugged off his unpleasant thoughts as Lucy's lovely face rose in his mind. Anxious to wed the wonderful Irish woman he was coming to care for a great deal, Sam clicked his tongue to the horse and started the trip to the church.

THE BRAND-NEW SPRUCE VALLEY CHRISTIAN CHURCH stood at the end of Spruce Street, the main road through town. The bright white building was an attractive structure with two stained-glass windows on either side of the front door and three more on each side. It had been built low to the ground to accommodate some of the elderly members of the congregation who had difficulties navigating steps.

There was only one low step onto the natural pine landing before entering through the red door into the small vestibule. Five rows of pews made of oak took up most of the sanctuary, but a small altar and three short pews for the choir were situated at the front of it.

As he entered it, Sam inhaled the scents of fragrant wood and the linseed oil that had been used to polish the pews and other things.

Paul stood at the altar, a fond smile on his face as Sam and Gray approached. "Well, Sam, ready for your big day?"

Sam nodded. "Yeah. I'm very lucky to be marrying a woman like Lucy."

"She is indeed a fine specimen of the fairer sex," Paul said. "I think you're well-matched."

"Thanks, Paul. I appreciate that." Sam looked toward the door. "I hope it won't be long before she arrives."

Gray chuckled. "Impatient, are we? Perhaps you're thinking of the wedding night."

Sam gave him a sharp glance and a disapproving frown settled on Paul's features.

However, this had no effect on Gray, who just shrugged. "Don't act like it hadn't crossed your mind, Sam."

Sam's scowl deepened. "This isn't the place or time to discuss that."

Gray grinned. "My apologies," he said, but didn't sound contrite in the least.

Choosing to ignore him, Sam asked Paul how he liked the church and they talked about other town matters while they waited.

SITTING behind Mason and Jenny in their buggy, Lucy fought back panic as the church came into sight. It wasn't far from the Inn, but Jenny had insisted that Lucy wasn't going to risk getting her dress dirty by walking. As she watched the married couple, it was easy to see the love they shared, and Lucy prayed that it would be the same for her and Sam.

*No, it will be,* she told herself in a stern tone. *Stop acting like an igit and more like the mature, confident woman ye are.* Her emotions in check, she started looking forward to the wedding, and grew eager to see Sam.

They stopped before the church and Mason helped both women out of the buggy. Lucy smoothed her dress and clutched the pretty spring bouquet of flowers Jenny had bought for her at Frost's store. She held it to her nose and inhaled. The floral fragrances further calmed her nerves. Mason had graciously agreed to walk Lucy down the aisle, and she was glad for his strong arm as they stepped into the church.

Someone had gone ahead of them, and Wade Bannon, whom Lucy had only met yesterday, began playing a pretty song on his harpsichord.

After a few moments, Mason smiled down at her. "Ready?"

Lucy clutched his arm a little tighter and squared her shoulders. "Aye, I am."

Mason led her into the sanctuary and the guests who'd gathered stood. Murmurs of admiration of Lucy's appearance rippled through the crowd, but the only person's opinion she cared about was Sam's.

Her gaze came to rest on him and her breathing quickened. He looked splendid in the deep navy suit that made his blue eyes look even more vivid. His blond hair was combed back, and he was clean-shaven, emphasizing his strong jaw. His gaze roamed over her and heat rose in her cheeks as she saw desire in his eyes. Relief that he found her appearance pleasing made her feel buoyant.

Paul smiled at her and began the service. "Dearly beloved, we are gathered here today in the sight of God to witness the union of Mr. Samuel Slater and Miss Lucy Magee." He looked at Mason. "Who gives this woman to be wed?"

"I do."

"Very well."

With a grin, Mason handed Lucy off to Sam. "Be good to her."

Lucy's pulse skipped as Sam's warm hands closed around hers.

Sam sobered. "I will."

During the brief ceremony, Lucy concentrated on her vows, but it was difficult when Sam was holding her hands and meeting her gaze. He seemed to fill her vision, and she almost forgot that they were in a church and that they had an audience. When Sam slipped a gold band on her finger, she felt an odd sense of homecoming.

Her mother had taught her to listen to her intuition, and she heeded that advice now. *You've found your destiny*, a voice whispered in her mind. She watched Sam slide the ring home and smiled up at him as happiness flowed through her.

They might not be in love, but they liked and respected each other. Their attraction to each other was evident, too. Lucy was honest and admitted to herself that being that far along in their relationship was more than she'd expected, and it gave her hope that perhaps love would come.

When Paul pronounced them man and wife and gave Sam permission to kiss her, a jolt of awareness ran through Lucy. He lowered his head and pressed his lips firmly to hers. The kiss they shared couldn't be called chaste, but it was still respectable. Sam drew back before Lucy was ready for the kiss to end, and the heat in Sam's gaze said that he felt the same way.

Paul presented them to the congregation, and they walked up the aisle while the congregation applauded.

As they emerged from the church, bright sunlight shone down on them, and it seemed to Lucy that it was an omen for their future.

# CHAPTER 10

*L*ater that afternoon, as she rode beside Sam in the buggy on their way to his ranch, it struck Lucy that it was now her home, too. She and Greta had brought the rest of her belongings out the day before, leaving just what she'd need for today in her room at the Inn. Her single small suitcase was stashed at the back of their seat.

Nerves fluttered in Lucy's stomach as she thought ahead to the wedding night. Sam had told her that he didn't expect her to be ready to engage in relations, but she wondered if it was wise to delay consummating their union. The thought of it filled her with uncertainty and excitement in equal measure. A couple of her married cousins had educated her about what happened in the marital bed. However, being told and participating in the act were two very different things.

To distract herself, she turned her attention to their surroundings. A pair of squirrels scurried up a tree, chattering as they went. Several crows flew overhead, calling out to each other in their raucous voices. However, even as she noted all of this, she was still acutely aware of Sam's presence beside her.

"Did you enjoy the reception?"

Sam's voice made Lucy jump a little. "I did. It was lovely. Did you have a good time?"

He grinned. "Yes. The food was delicious, but my favorite part was the dancing. Especially the songs where I was able to hold you closer."

"Aye. That was my favorite part, too," Lucy agreed.

His half-smile sent her pulse skipping along. "Glad to hear it."

Lucy glanced at the large basket that sat behind the seat. "It was kind of everyone to send food home with us. There's so much of it. We should share it with our ranch hands, so it doesn't go bad in the heat."

"About that. A few weeks ago, I ordered an icebox for us. It should arrive next week sometime," Sam said.

Lucy stared at him agog for several moments before speaking. "Sam! Iceboxes are terribly expensive! You shouldn't have done that. Ye've already spent so much on outfitting the kitchen so nicely."

Sam took her hand and kissed it. "Lucy, I promise you that if I hadn't had the money, I wouldn't have spent it. It's a practical purchase as well as adding efficiency to our lives. Eddie Carmichael started an ice delivery business last winter and I think we should take advantage of his services. He travels into the mountains close by where there's plenty of ice to harvest. It's actually turned into quite a lucrative endeavor for him."

Lucy's mind started running through all the ways an icebox would improve their food storage. Milk and cream would stay fresh longer, as well as meat and desserts. It would be more convenient than running to the spring house every time she needed something.

"Do you want me to send it back?"

She snapped her gaze to his. "Of course, not! I was just surprised. Don't you dare return it!"

Sam's rich laugh rang out and he squeezed her hand. "I'm just teasing you. I wouldn't do that. It would cost an arm and a leg to ship."

Lucy nodded emphatically. "Right, so we'll be keeping it."

Sam chuckled and released her hand so he could turn their horse into their driveway. As they arrived at the barn, one of the ranch hands who'd stayed behind to do the daily chores approached them.

"Hello, Doc. Mrs. Slater. Congratulations on your nuptials."

"Thank you, Will," Sam said.

"I'll be happy to take care of the horse and buggy for you," Will said. "You newlyweds shouldn't have to do chores on your wedding day."

"We appreciate it," Lucy said.

They exited the buggy, and Lucy took the food basket while Sam grabbed her suitcase.

"Will, there's plenty of food here. I'll fix you a nice plate for supper," Lucy said. "It's only fair that you celebrate our day with us."

A broad smile spread across Will's face. "I'd enjoy that, ma'am."

"All right, then. Come to the house in about half an hour."

Will touched the brim of his hat and led their horse away.

"That was very nice of you," Sam said, offering his arm to Lucy.

She tucked her hand into the crook of his elbow, and they started toward the house. "I want your ranch hands to like me and I want to get to know them. It's important to be on good terms with them."

"I'm of the same mind. I find that happy employees work harder than those who are treated poorly," Sam commented. "That said, if any of the men become overly friendly with you, be sure to tell me."

Lucy raised an eyebrow as they reached the kitchen door. "I'll tell ya, but not until I've taken care of the problem myself."

With a haughty air, she opened the door and went inside, while Sam grinned and followed her.

Lucy stood at the kitchen sink, washing the plates that Will had brought back once he'd finished with them. She started when strong arms slipped around her waist.

"Hello, wife."

Lucy smiled upon recognizing Sam's voice next to her ear.

A rush of emotion ran through at hearing him use that term for the first time. "Hello, husband."

Sam drew her back against him and nuzzled her neck. "That has such a nice ring to it."

"Aye, it does." The contact with his strong body made her stomach flip pleasantly.

"This is our wedding night. You shouldn't be doing dishes."

"I know, but I just couldn't leave them until morning."

Sam chuckled. "Spoken like a true homemaker. Tell me, Lucy, how much did those Irish brothers of yours corrupt you?"

Lucy grinned as she rinsed the last dish and started drying it. "I don't think I should answer that question. You might be shocked."

"Mmm. A lady of mystery. Tell me this much, did their corruption include playing cards?"

Lucy set the plate aside and turned in his arms. "Why don't ya get a deck and we'll find out?"

He flashed a grin at her, pressed a firm kiss to her lips, and left the kitchen. She smiled and glanced at the cabinet where Sam kept his bourbon. Did she dare? Deciding to risk it, she got out two tumblers and the liquor. She set them on the table and sat down to wait.

Sam returned with a deck of cards, a tablet and pencil for keeping score. He pulled up a chair and sat down.

Lucy saw him glance at the decanter and tumblers. "I don't imbibe often, but today is a special day, so I see nothing wrong with have a wee bit."

"I assure you that I don't think less of you for it."

"Thank you. While I'm being honest, I've also never gone further than kissing a few men," Lucy said. "I'm not a loose woman, but I have taken that small liberty."

Sam grinned. "Frankly, I'd be surprised if someone as beautiful as you hadn't been kissed before. I suspected as much, since you're so good at it."

Her face turned pink as she laughed. "I'm glad ya think so."

"I do. I like this rather naughty side of you. Makes me wonder what other secrets you may be hiding."

Lucy sent him a coy look. "Nothing too scandalous, but I might have a few more surprises for you."

"I look forward to discovering them." He lifted his glass. "I'd like to propose a toast."

Lucy said, "I agree. To what shall we toast?"

"A bright future filled with happiness, good health, and prosperity."

"And as many babies as the Good Lord blesses us with," Lucy added. "*Sláinte!*"

"*Sláinte!*"

They clinked their glasses together and downed the half-finger Lucy had poured for them. Warmth spread through Lucy, making her smile.

Sam held out the deck to her. "You cut."

Lucy did and asked, "What are we playing?"

"You tell me."

After a moment, she replied, "Gin rummy."

"Aha. I had a hunch you were a card player."

"Aye."

Sam dealt the cards and the game began. They played for the next hour and a half, exchanging good-natured barbs and laughing. Lucy came out the victor, winning most of the hands, and Sam admitted defeat.

As he gathered up the cards, he said, "I'd say that you excelled in your card game education. You're a formidable opponent."

"Aye. I don't mean to sound conceited, but my brothers don't like to play me much anymore because I rarely lose."

Sam's eyebrows lifted. "Really?"

"Really."

"Did you let me win?"

"Nay. I don't believe in doing that," Lucy replied.

"Good. I prefer to win on my own merits, not because an opponent throws the game out of pity."

Lucy rose from the table, took their glasses to the sink, and put the bourbon away. "Your integrity is one of the things I like most about you, Sam."

She returned to him and surprised them both by sitting on his lap. Yes, the alcohol had perhaps relaxed her inhibitions a bit, but Lucy was honest with herself and admitted that she wanted to be close to Sam. Since they were married now, there was no shame in being physical with him.

Sam slid his arms around her waist. "What else do you like about me?"

Brushing a golden lock of hair from his forehead, she replied, "I admire your intelligence and sense of humor. Your kind and generous, and so very handsome."

He smiled and Lucy's pulse skipped. "It's good to know that you think so highly of me."

She trailed a fingertip down his cheek and traced his lightly stubbled jaw. "If I didn't, I wouldn't have married ya. I would never settle for any man who didn't meet my standards."

His eyes darkened with desire. "I'm very fortunate to have met them."

Feeling his strong body pressed against hers excited Lucy, and she wanted to kiss him. Running her hand around to the back of his neck, she urged him closer. He obliged and her eyes closed as he claimed her mouth in a kiss that spread heat through her body. Sam held her closer, and Lucy wound her arms around his neck, inviting him to deepen the kiss. He melded his mouth to hers, making her breathing quicken as he caressed her back.

SAM ALLOWED himself to become lost in Lucy. He drank deeply from her soft, pliant lips and reveled in the way she felt in his arms. The whiskey on her lips only enhanced her delicious taste and he couldn't get enough.

Lucy's hair was still up in the beautiful braided bun. Sam started pulling out the pins holding it in place and placed them on the table. He wanted to see her ebony tresses free and loose around her shoulders.

One became snagged and he pulled a trifle too hard. Lucy let out a soft yelp and broke the kiss.

"Sorry about that," Sam said with a wry smile.

"That's all right."

Sam took a deep breath. "Perhaps it's for the best. I was carried away again."

Goosebumps spread over his shoulders as she threaded her fingers through the hair at his temples. "There's no need to apologize. We're married now."

"Yes, but we agreed to take things slow since we're not well acquainted yet."

Hesitation flitted across her face and her brow puckered as her eyes met his. "I know that's what we decided, but I've changed my mind."

Although Sam wanted to make love with Lucy, he was concerned that she was making a hasty decision. "I don't want you to rush into anything and then regret it."

Lucy cupped his cheek. "I know my own mind, and I won't regret it."

When she pressed her lips to his, Sam's resistance faded away. The passionate way she kissed him convinced him that she was truly ready to become husband and wife in every way. Gathering her close, Sam stood with Lucy in his arms, and carried her to his bedroom.

He set Lucy on her feet and took her face in his hands. "Are you absolutely certain?"

Resting her hands onto Sam's chest, Lucy's gaze didn't waver as her eyes met his. "I'm positive, Sam. Make love to me."

Hearing those words sent heat surging through his veins and he couldn't refuse her request. He wanted her too much. Pulling her against him, he kissed her with urgency, unable to hold back any longer. Unwilling to break contact with Lucy, Sam kicked the bedroom door shut.

Amid heated kisses and whispered words of affection and passion, they were carried away on a powerful current of sensual pleasure. The moon was low on its zenith before they were sated and drifted into a contented slumber, still wrapped in each other's arms.

# CHAPTER 11

The aromas of coffee and frying sausage woke Sam the next morning. Opening his eyes, he discovered that he was alone in his bed. He surmised that Lucy must be cooking breakfast as he stretched. Rising from the bed, he dressed in an older pair of black trousers and a gray shirt. He combed his hair and headed for the kitchen. His stomach rumbled as the smell of food grew stronger.

Entering the kitchen, he saw Lucy stirring some kind of batter in a bowl. She caught sight of him and the smile that lit her face made his heartbeat throb in his chest. She'd pulled her hair back on the sides, but otherwise, it cascaded down her back. The memory of how silky it felt when he'd buried his fingers in the gorgeous locks hit Sam like a hammer and he wanted to drag her back to bed.

"Good morning," she greeted him. "Did you sleep well?"

The mischievous sparkle in her eyes made Sam laugh. "I certainly did. How about you?"

"Very well, indeed." She went to the stove where a second frying pan sat. "How many pancakes would you like?"

Sam's mouth watered as he looked at the other pan that contained browned sausage links. "I'll start with four and go from there."

Lucy started pouring batter into the frying pan. "I'm glad you have a good appetite. I'm used to cooking for a lot of people."

Sam came over and filled his coffee cup from the pot. "Well, I'll do my best to keep you in practice for when we have a big family of our own."

Lucy smiled up at him. "Aye. I don't think I'll forget how to since I'll be cooking for the ranch hands, too."

A confused frown settled on Sam's features. "For the ranch hands?"

Lucy nodded. "I understand that it's my responsibility to cook for them, and I'm sure they'll be glad for some good food instead of the things they make for themselves."

Sam wasn't aware that Lucy knew so much about the ranch hands. He realized that he had little idea what the men ate. Gray was a fairly competent cook, and he often made a meal for him and Sam. "You're planning to cook for them?"

"Of course. Don't other ranch wives feed the men?"

Sam took a sip of coffee and smiled at how good it tasted. It was much better than his. He got back to the matter at hand. "Who told you that?"

Lucy glanced at him before flipping a pancake. "Greta and Jenny. You don't seem to approve of the idea."

Her tone made Sam tread carefully. The last thing he wanted was to argue the morning after their wedding. "It's just that we don't have a cookhouse."

His mouth watered as she placed a big stack of pancakes and sausage on a plate. "Not yet, but our table is plenty big enough since we only have four hands. We can build a cookhouse later when we have more money, but for now, they can eat here."

Carrying the plate she'd handed him to the table, Sam realized that other than Gray, he didn't know his employees very well. In fact, there were days when Sam didn't see any of the hands, even on paydays. Sam gave Gray the money, and he doled out the wages. Wouldn't it be a good idea to know more about his men? Especially with all the disturbing events lately?

As he sat down, a chill ran through Sam. Could one of the men be behind it all? As he took a sip of coffee, Sam decided to talk to Gray to get his opinion on the matter.

He looked at Lucy. "You're right. The men should eat with us. I'll tell Gray that they're to come to breakfast the day after tomorrow." He gave her a seductive smile. "We may not be able to take a honeymoon, but I'd like you to myself a little longer."

Lucy filled her plate and came over to the table. Before sitting down, she planted a lingering kiss on his lips. "I like the way you think. Now, eat your breakfast before it gets cold."

Sam chuckled. "Yes, ma'am."

OVER THE NEXT FEW DAYS, Lucy started settling in and making their house a true home. Sam had surprised her with a brand-new sewing machine, which they'd set up in her old room. All her belongings had been moved to her and Sam's room.

On the second day, after she'd cooked for the ranch hands, she finished cleaning up from breakfast and made new curtains for the kitchen. She'd decided on a blue floral print that was pretty, but not too feminine. As she brought the curtains out to the kitchen, Sam arrived home. He'd gone to his office to see a few patients.

"Oh, good. You can help me," Lucy said when he entered the kitchen.

He smiled and kissed her cheek. "Hello to you, too."

Lucy chuckled and kissed him back. "Hello. How were your patients?"

It had been a frustrating afternoon for Sam, but just the sight of Lucy washed much of his irritation away. Her eyes sparkled with good humor, and her pretty smile made him want to kiss much more than just her cheek.

"I've had better days, but that's over now."

Lucy's brow creased. "What happened?"

Sam blew out a breath and went to the sink to wash his hands. "Sometimes I wonder why people seek out treatment when they won't heed my instructions."

"That doesn't make much sense," Lucy agreed. "Did they say why they didn't listen?"

Sam leaned a hip on the sink as he dried his hands. "Zacharia Welliver is a rather stubborn old man and he seems to just like complaining. He has bunions, but he won't soak his feet with the salts I've prescribed."

"He sounds like my father. Ya often have ta challenge him before he'll do something," Lucy said. "Or make him think it was his idea all along."

Sam shook his head. "I'm afraid I'm not much good at that sort of thing."

Lucy sent him a coy look. "That's what ya have me for. What does he do for a livin'?"

"Well, he used to be a furniture maker, but his bad feet have made it hard for him to do that sort of work anymore."

"Does he have a shop?"

"Yeah. It's not far from the station. Why?"

Lucy looked over at one corner of the kitchen. "We need a corner china cupboard. I'll pay him a visit when I go to town with ye tomorrow."

Sam cocked an eyebrow. "You're going to see him?"

"Aye. We women have a way of bringin' men around to our way of thinkin'."

The alluring way she looked at him sent his blood through his veins faster. "Oh, yes. I know what wily creatures females are."

Lucy's pretty laughter filled the kitchen. "Da used to say the same thing to Ma." She patted Sam's arm. "Don't worry. I'll make Mr. Welliver see the light. Just leave it to me."

Although he was curious about how she was going to handle Zachariah, Sam knew that she wasn't going to tell him. He'd have to wait to find out. "All right, but don't let him overcharge you for the cupboard."

A sly smile curved her mouth. "Don't worry, Sam. Ma and Da taught all us children how to haggle. Mr. Welliver won't pull the wool over my eyes."

"I don't doubt it." Sam eyed the material laying on the table. "What's all this?"

"They're the curtains I made for the kitchen today. Will ya help me hang them?"

Sam nodded. "I'd be happy to. You'll have direct me, though, because I haven't the foggiest notion how to go about it."

"It'll be my pleasure."

Sam grinned as she started instructing him on the proper way to hang the curtains. As they worked, he discovered that she was quite particular about how it was done. He learned more about hanging curtains than he'd ever wanted to, but he also had a good time.

When they finished, Sam stood back, going over their work with a critical eye. Although he didn't know the intricacies of sewing or drapery, Lucy's café-style curtains rivaled anything he'd ever seen. They brightened the room, yet they weren't offensive to his masculine sensibilities.

The bottom panels could be drawn at night for privacy but opened during the day to admit light. They also added a touch of elegance, and Sam was proud to have married a woman with such talent.

"You do very fine work, indeed, Lucy. With your kind of skill, I predict that your future dressmaking business will be a success," he said.

Her proud smile warmed Sam's heart. "Thank you. I'm so happy that you like them."

"I do. Very much."

"I appreciate your help," Lucy said.

"You're welcome."

Lucy admired the curtains for a moment before moving to the stove. "I have a chicken in the oven with roasted potatoes and carrots."

Sam's mouth watered as her words made him aware of the savory aromas filling the kitchen. "It smells delicious."

"It won't be ready for a while. Would you care for something to tide ye over?"

Sam was about to respond until he saw the gleam in her eyes. Her tempting smile whet his appetite, but not for food. A different type of hunger assailed him as she exited the kitchen. She hummed a faint tune as she walked down the hallway. It beckoned to him and he was powerless to resist its pull. It was only a few moments before he followed his wife.

A COUPLE OF DAYS LATER, Lucy woke near dawn. A feeling of unease slid through her as she glanced at the window. The sky outside had just begun to lighten, the color somewhere between indigo and blue. Her gaze turned to Sam, who still slept. She smiled for a moment before getting out of bed, careful not to disturb Sam. He hadn't gotten home until late the previous evening and he needed his rest.

Lucy donned her robe and left their room. She yawned as she padded out to the kitchen to start the fire in the cookstove. Once she had it going, she put a kettle on to heat while she went to dress. Tiptoeing into their room, Lucy was glad to see that Sam still slept. The first golden rays of dawn lit the room, illuminating his handsome face.

She watched him the entire time she donned her undergarments and a deep-blue cotton dress with white lace at the collar and wrists. It wasn't the prettiest dress, but Lucy was learning that function was more important in her new life than fashion. You couldn't gather eggs or milk a cow in a fancy gown. Once she was dressed, she pulled her hair back and wound it into a low bun. Finished, she headed back to the kitchen.

The kettle wasn't quite ready, so Lucy decided to go gather the eggs. Debating what to make for breakfast that morning, she got her egg basket and opened the kitchen door. Horror at the scene before her froze Lucy where she stood.

Three mutilated sheep lay on the porch. Pools of still congealing blood spread out from under their bodies, seeping into the floorboards. Their wide, staring eyes conveyed the fear they'd felt before being slaughtered.

The egg basket fell from Lucy's loosened grasp. Her breathing became ragged as she stared at the carnage. It was several moments before she reacted. A scream rose from deep inside her and burst forth, cutting through the early morning quiet.

SAM JERKED awake at the sound of a woman screaming. His heart started pounding as he sat up, looking for Lucy. The screaming continued, growing louder. He jumped out of bed and ran through the house, dressed only in his union suit. Entering the kitchen, he found Lucy standing in the kitchen doorway.

When she screamed again, he rushed to her and looked over her shoulder to see what was frightening her so much. A jolt of shock rushed through him as he saw the dead, bloodied sheep on the porch.

He wrapped his arms around Lucy from behind. "Sweet-heart, it's all right. Shh. I'm here. It's all right."

With a sob, Lucy turned and wrapped her arms around Sam so hard it made him grunt. He held her close, caressing her back and reassuring her.

After a few minutes, she quieted and sniffed before pulling back to look up at him. Her eyes swam with tears and her nose had turned red.

"Oh, Sam, who would do such a thing?" she asked.

He cupped her face. "I don't know, but we'll get to the bottom of it. Come away from here."

Lucy nodded and let him lead her to the table. He pulled out a chair for her and she sat down. The kettle started whistling, but it didn't seem to register with her. Sam took it off the stove and fixed a cup of tea with a small dose of whiskey in it. He could give her a sedative if necessary, but he hoped the alcohol would help calm her nerves.

"Stay here and drink this. I'll deal with...that," he said.

Her expression blank, Lucy nodded and took a sip of the hot tea. A slight grimace crossed her face, but she took a second sip. Sam left her to finish her drink and stepped outside. Looking over the sheep, he saw that their throats had been slit and their stomachs slashed open.

Hot rage burned through Sam as he gazed at them. Not only had the culprits killed three good ewes, but their new lambs were now orphans. They would have to be hand fed. Worse than all of that, though, was the blatant attempt to scare them. It rankled further to know that they'd succeeded. Lucy was in shock over the incident.

A breeze rose and something on one of the sheep's back fluttered. Avoiding blood, Sam moved closer and saw that the object was a note. Snatching it from the pin that had been stuck in the ewe's thick wool, he read it.

*This land is cursed. No good will come to whoever stays here. Move on before someone gets hurt.*

Although tempted to crush the note, Sam refrained. Taking a couple of deep breaths to quell his anger, he folded it and tried to put it in his pocket, but then realized that he wasn't dressed. Scrubbing a hand over his face, he rose and went inside.

Lucy had finished her tea and although pale, her tears had stopped, and she appeared to have gathered herself. He had no wish to upset her again, but it was necessary to show her the note.

Sam sat next to her and held it out to her. "This was left on one of the ewes."

Lucy raised questioning eyes to him before taking it. Her mouth thinned and color rose in her cheeks as she read the missive. Her nostrils flared as her chest rose and fell rapidly. Sam jumped when she slammed a fist down on the table, hard enough to make her empty cup rattle where it sat.

"I'll not have it! I won't tolerate cowardly evildoers skulking about, killing our sheep and leavin' them on our stoop!" She glared at Sam, her eyes blazing like lightning flashing through rolling gray clouds. "They're just tryin' to scare us, scare *me*, is more like it." Lucy stood and paced to the door, throwing it open.

Sam followed her when she strode out onto the porch, passing the carnage with only a quick glance. "Lucy, where are you going? Come back inside until we get this cleaned up."

Ignoring him, Lucy shouted, "Whoever you are, whoever is responsible for this, your wastin' your time!" She pointed at the porch. "It'll take much more than a few dead sheep to scare me. I'm not a woman of faint heart! Nay, I've more courage in my wee little finger than the whole lot of you put together!"

Sam doubted that the criminals were anywhere near the ranch, but he admired Lucy's courage, nonetheless. "While I agree with you on that, wife, I believe you're wasting your breath. I doubt the miscreants hung around."

Lucy turned to him with a haughty expression. "I'm not daft, Sam. It just made me feel better."

Sam laughed and took her by the shoulders. "That's my feisty Irish lass. You're one of the bravest women I've ever met. Now, would you please go back inside? I'll go get Gray, and one of the other men, and we'll get this cleaned up."

Lucy planted her hands on her hips. "We might as well butcher these three. No sense letting the meat or wool go to waste. I'll go change into my old clothes, and we can get started."

She rose up on tiptoe, pressed a kiss to his cheek, and went inside. With an amused shake of his head, Sam went to go find Gray.

# CHAPTER 12

*L*ater that morning, Sam and Gray were on their way to see Drake when they met him halfway there.

As they all reined their mounts to a stop, Sam noted the dark expression on Drake's face. "I see that you already know what happened this morning."

Drake gave him a brisk nod. "I'm not sure exactly what you're talking about, but three ewes are missing. I know because three lambs kept trying to nurse from ewes that aren't their mothers."

"How do you know they're not their mothers?" Sam asked.

One side of Drake's mouth lifted. "The ewes refused these other lambs, which they do when the lamb is not theirs."

"Oh, I see."

Sam made a mental note to endeavor to learn more about raising sheep. He'd left such matters to Ernie and Gray, but he felt a little embarrassed that as the owner of a sheep ranch, he didn't know such a simple fact about sheep behavior. His consternation grew when he noticed Drake and Gray exchange an amused glance.

He sat a little straighter in his saddle. "If you two are done making fun of me, I'd like to fill Drake in about what happened at home this morning."

"Yes, of course," Gray said, but he didn't sound contrite at all.

Sam ignored his annoyance and related the incident to Drake. The young man stayed silent during the story and didn't speak for a couple of moments after Sam had finished.

"Did anything odd happen last night?" Sam prompted when Drake's silence stretched on.

Drake shook his head. "No. The sheep weren't restless, and the dogs didn't raise a ruckus, either." Anger flared in Drake's eyes. "Whoever did this knows our dogs, and how to move sheep so they stay calm."

"Who was on duty last night?" Gray asked.

"Me. It was quiet all night."

"And you didn't fall asleep even briefly?"

Drake bristled at Gray's question. "I was awake all night. I don't shirk my work."

"Gray wasn't suggesting you did," Sam said. "Staying up all night is hard. It wouldn't be surprising if you dozed off a little."

"Well, I didn't," Drake insisted.

"All right. I believe you," Sam responded. "We need to list everyone who knows the herd and is familiar with the dogs."

Gray said, "That may be a long list. Ernie had a lot of friends who used to visit him. I'm sure the dogs were familiar with them, too."

Sam sighed. "I know, but we need to start somewhere. Lucy was scared to death this morning. I won't stand for her being upset like that. Josh needs a list so he knows who to interrogate." He looked at Drake. "Come to the house. The three of us can work on it together, and I'll take it to Josh."

Drake nodded. "Good idea."

The three men turned their horses around and took off for the ranch.

JOSH'S GAZE moved down the paper over the list of names that Sam had brought. He scratched his head. It was going to take him a month to talk to all the people on it. He hadn't socialized with Ernie much, so he hadn't realized he knew so many people.

He blew out a breath and looked over at Sam. "Seems like Ernie knew half the town."

Sam smiled. "Those are just the people we know about."

"It's a lot of people to talk to."

"Well, I'm thinking that we can probably cross off the women and children," Sam said.

Josh shook his head. "No, we can't. They may not have done the deed, but it's possible that they're witnesses, or that they overheard something."

"Oh. I hadn't thought of that."

Tapping the badge on his chest, Josh grinned. "That's why I'm the sheriff and you're not."

Sam chuckled. "Too true. How will you go about narrowing down that list?"

Rubbing his jaw, Josh went over various options in his mind. A crafty smile spread over his face. "I know exactly what I'll do."

"Care to share?" Sam asked.

"Not yet. I have to work out a few details."

"Very well. I'll leave it in your capable hands." Sam rose from the chair on the other side of Josh's desk. "Keep me posted."

"You know I will. Hey, it might not be a bad idea to have Grant stay at your place to keep watch on Lucy when no one else is around."

Sam had been thinking much along the same lines, but he wasn't sure he could afford to pay another employee. He'd have to go over his finances again. Then there was the issue of convincing Lucy. She was a proud woman, and he had a hunch that she would balk at the idea of having a bodyguard. After her shouted challenge to the miscreants, she'd set about sheering and butchering the sheep.

Sam might not know a lot about sheep behavior, but he was proficient at butchering. He'd instructed Lucy on the process and she'd caught on quick. They'd kept out a nice piece of roast, put some in the smokehouse, and stored some in barrels to salt cure. They'd have plenty of meat for a while, and Lucy had stated that she knew many ways to prepare it so that they didn't become bored with the mutton.

Coming out of his musings, Sam said, "That's a good idea. Any idea where I can find him?"

"Well, he always has lunch at the Inn, so I'm guessing that's where he is now."

Sam thanked Josh and went on his way. Before heading to the Inn, he stopped at his office. He kept two identical sets of financial ledgers—one at the office and one at home.

When he first started his practice, Sam had had a weather resistant box made with a slot in the top. He'd mounted it next to the door and tied a pencil and small tablet to it so people could leave him a message when he wasn't there. He checked the box and was glad it was empty.

After reviewing the ledger, he determined that he could afford to offer Grant a small stipend along with room and board.

That decided, he went to the Inn and was glad to find Grant just finishing his meal.

"Hello Grant. Mind if I sit down?" he asked.

"Not at all." He motioned to a chair.

Sam took it and asked, "Are you employed right now?"

Grant replied, "Not right now.. Why?"

"I was wondering if you would guard Lucy. I wish it was more, but the most I can afford to pay you is two dollars and forty cents per week along with room and board."

Grant took a sip of coffee and leaned back in his chair. "That's acceptable. I could save up for a new horse since I wouldn't have to pay for lodging." His brows drew together. "My horse got pneumonia on the way here a couple of weeks ago and couldn't be saved. I was on my way to Helena. No one has been going there as of late, and I don't have enough funds to buy a quality horse that has good stamina."

Sam nodded. "Yes. A good horse is a necessity for anyone traveling long distances."

"I could walk, but a man walking alone is much more vulnerable than a man riding alone," Grant commented. "It would also take me much longer to get there."

"Right." Sam sighed. "We had an incident this morning, which prompted me to offer you this position."

"What kind of incident?" After Sam's brief rundown of the situation, Grant asked, "When would you like me to start?"

"Is tomorrow too soon?" Sam asked. "You're welcome to come get settled this evening, if you like."

Grant finished his coffee before answering. "I'll take you up on that. Then I could start first thing in the morning and get acquainted with the other men."

"I'll be in town until late this afternoon. I have my buggy, so you could ride home with me."

Grant smiled. "Much obliged, Sam."

Sam stood. "Happy to do it, and thanks for agreeing to help us."

The men bid each other farewell and Sam left to go tend a few of his shut-in patients. As he made his rounds, Sam felt lighter in knowing that Grant would keep Lucy safe. He only hoped that his new wife would agree with the plan he'd already set in motion.

～

LUCY'S EYES glittered with anger as she looked at her husband. Her face grew hot and she planted her hands on her hips. "You did *what?*"

Sam pursed his lips for a moment before replying. "You heard me. I hired Grant for security of the ranch."

A derisive snort escaped Lucy as she moved to the stove. "Ya hired him to babysit me, is what ya mean." She turned her attention to taking the mutton roast out of the oven. "I can take care of myself, Sam. You taught me how to shoot, and I keep my derringer in my skirt pocket now. Plus, I'm good with kitchen knives." The smile that tugged at Sam's mouth irritated Lucy further. "Do ye find that funny?" she challenged.

Sam sobered. "No. Well, maybe a little. I know how fierce you are. You kept Gray at bay with a knife, but the fact is that I doubt you could fend off more than one man. Grant will be here to give all of us peace of mind."

His sincerity soothed her ruffled feathers a little. "So, he won't be here just to watch over me?"

"I won't lie to you. That will be his main priority, but only when the rest of us can't be with you. Other times, he'll be patrolling and guarding the ranch," Sam replied.

Lucy lifted the roaster from the oven and was happy with the way the meat looked. As she tested the potatoes and carrots to make sure they were done, she thought about the situation. Although it rankled that Sam thought she couldn't defend herself, she admitted that he was right about not being able to fend off more than one attacker.

She replaced the lid and started setting the table. Sam still stood there, waiting for a response.

When she was done with the dishes, she said, "I suppose it's not a bad idea to have Grant here. Maybe he can catch whoever is doing all this."

Stepping closer, Sam put his hands on her shoulders. "Precisely my thinking. I need to know that you're safe, Lucy. I care for you a great deal, and I'd be devastated if something happened to you. I'm your husband. It's my duty to protect you."

The concern and affection in his eyes melted Lucy's anger away. "I care for you, too, Sam. I'm sorry I was testy. I hate to admit it, but knowing that Grant is watching over me will give me some peace of mind."

Sam slid his hands up to cup her face. "Good. Thank you."

His touch stirred Lucy's senses and a shiver ran through her as he stroked a thumb over her cheek. Her lips parted when his eyes lowered to her mouth. She now craved his kisses and caresses, and Lucy found herself daydreaming about making love with Sam.

The need to kiss him grew. She rested her hands on his chest and rose on tiptoe as he dipped his head. Their lips touched and instant fire flared inside. She pressed against him and slid a hand up to play with the hair at the nape of his neck. His growl of pleasure increased her ardor and she wanted to drag him off to their bedroom.

A rap on the door made Lucy squeal in surprise, and she pulled out of Sam's embrace. She giggled at his wicked smile as she straightened her apron. "That'll be the men. I'm sure they're famished. Would you please answer the door while I finish supper, Sam?"

"As you wish, milady," Sam replied.

Several men filed over the threshold when Sam opened the door. Jensen Davis, a grizzled, white-haired old-timer, smiled at Lucy and took a seat.

On the first day, Lucy had informed the men that they weren't to wait to sit down until she did, since she would be finishing up getting the food to the table. Although they'd agreed to that, they still insisted on waiting to begin eating until she sat down.

"Miss Lucy, the good smells coming from the house have been making my mouth water all day," Tom Barker informed her.

Lucy smiled at him as she sat a large bowl of potatoes on the table. "I hope it tastes as good as it smells."

Tom appeared to be somewhere in his thirties. His hazel eyes crinkled at the corners and his close-cropped, light brown hair stuck up in some places. "I'm sure it's even better," he remarked.

Lucy was surprised to see Grant enter the kitchen next. He looked at Sam, who just shrugged sheepishly. Apparently, her husband had already decided the matter of hiring Grant and talking to her had just been a mere formality.

She flashed an angry look at Sam but gave Grant a warm greeting. "It's very nice to see you again, Grant. It's grand to have you with us."

Grant's gaze moved between her and Sam, and he gave her a wry smile. "It's good to be here, ma'am, but I take it that you're a little surprised to see me."

"Just a tad, but it's a nice surprise," Lucy assured him.

"Methinks someone may be in the doghouse," Gray quipped, bringing up the rear.

Lucy pretended not to hear him as she turned back to the stove to retrieve the roast. Sam offered to take it to the table, but she ignored him and placed it in the center herself. He must've taken the hint because he sat in his customary seat at the head of the table.

Gray insisted on helping her finish up, and she thanked him warmly. The look of consternation on Sam's face gave her great satisfaction, as did the way Gray seemed to delight in needling his friend. She even allowed Gray to seat her, which turned Sam's expression even darker.

"Now then, would you please say grace for us, Jensen?"

The older man was taken aback by her request. "Um, well, sure, I guess. It's been a mighty long time since I did, so you'll have to pardon me if I fumble around a bit."

"You might be a bit rusty, but I'm certain ye'll do a fine job of it," Lucy said.

Jensen cleared his throat a couple of times. "Dear Lord, thanks for these fine vittles and the hands that made 'em. We're grateful for Miss Lucy's food, which is a heap better than the slop we been eating. Amen."

Lucy had to keep her head bowed a few moments longer to hide her amusement over Jensen's crude prayer. Raising her head, she said, "Thank you, Jensen. T'was very nice."

Jensen's self-conscious smile had a touch of pride to it, and Lucy was glad she'd asked him to say grace. "You're welcome, ma'am."

"Now then, let's eat before it gets cold," Lucy said.

The men didn't have to be told twice. Their plates were soon filled, and silence descended over the table for several minutes while everyone tucked into their meal. Lucy glanced at Sam a couple of times but didn't speak to him.

Lucy disliked being cross with Sam, but she couldn't help it. It hurt that he'd already made the decision to hire Grant before he'd talked to her. He'd been trying to placate her by discussing it. She'd thought he was different than most other men who thought that women were empty-headed creatures. Those men believed that the female of the species was incapable of intelligent thought concerning anything except domestic matters.

It didn't take long for the food to disappear, which was a great compliment to Lucy. She enjoyed cooking for the ranch hands, and liked their company. Their banter amused her, and the stories they told about each other kept her entertained.

Throughout the meal, Lucy kept a pleasant demeanor, but inside she seethed with anger and frustration. She was relieved when supper was over, and the group broke up. The ranch hands each bid her goodnight and left, leaving her and Sam alone.

Lucy busied herself cleaning up the kitchen. She put water on to heat for washing the dishes.

"All right. Let me have it, Lucy," Sam said as she turned back to the counter.

She kept her attention on her work, scraping the few scraps left on plates into a small bucket. "Let ya have it? What for?"

"You know perfectly well what for."

Lucy darted a glance at him. "You mean for discussing

something with me *after* ye've already made the decision for me? Or maybe it's for treatin' me like I haven't got a brain in my head? For being just as boorish and condescending to women as any other man?"

Sam's sigh drew her eyes to him. "Lucy, be reasonable. I was just thinking of your safety."

Incensed, Lucy speared him with a hard gaze. "Don't take that tone with me, Samuel Slater."

He lifted an eyebrow. "And what tone would that be?"

"Like I'm being daft or that I'm being difficult. Tell me something, would you treat a man the way you treated me today?" she inquired. Sam's gaze wavered and Lucy pounced. "Aha! I'm right. You wouldn't have gone behind their back and then tried to placate them! But ye'll do it to a woman."

"Lucy, please try to understand—"

"I understand just fine," Lucy interjected with an angry gesture. "I'm not stupid. I know that I wouldn't be able to fend off a man with sheer strength alone, but I do have a gun now. Even so, it's a good idea for Grant to be here, I know that.

"But you could've done me the courtesy of truly consulting me before just bringing Grant home. Instead, you made a pretense of it, almost as if you were mocking me. How would you feel if I did something like that to you?"

Sam sighed and rubbed the back of his neck. "I wouldn't like it at all. I'm sorry that it seemed like I slighted you, but it really was a matter of convenience. Grant doesn't have a horse right now, so it was easier if he came home with me. "If you had absolutely rejected the idea of hiring him, I would've taken him back into town. But if you did agree, then he would already be here so he could start tomorrow morning. I was just being practical."

The water on the stove started to boil. Lucy poured some into the big metal bowl she used to wash dishes while she thought about what Sam had said. She saw his logic and her irritation lowered a notch or two. Maybe Sam really hadn't meant to hurt her feelings. He'd never treated her with anything but kindness since they'd met.

"Perhaps you were, but you didn't mention that Grant was already here."

"A gross omission on my part, to be sure. I apologize."

Lucy narrowed her eyes at his conciliatory tone. "Do you mean that, or are you just trying to get back in my good graces?" Sam opened his mouth to answer but she held up a finger. "When Da angered Ma, they'd fight like wild cats, and then he would storm out of our flat," Lucy said. "Hours later, or perhaps the next morning, he'd come back and apologize. Sometimes he meant it, but most of the time he was just telling Ma what she wanted to hear, so she'd forgive him and get the fight over with.

"She usually gave in, even when she was in the right, just to create peace. I love Da. He's a good man, but he was of the mind that women should be obedient to their husbands and fathers.

"I believe women should respect men, but only when those men deserve it, Sam." She lifted her chin, her gaze never wavering. "Until today, I thought you a very rare man. Honest, loyal, and kind. The sort of man who valued a woman for more than her body or homemaking skills. A man I could always respect and trust. But now I wonder if I was wrong to hold ye in such high regard. So, which kind of man are ya, Sam? One like my father, or the kind I believed ya to be?" Sam saw the distrust in Lucy's eyes and it disturbed him. He knew that he had to proceed with caution. His instincts told him that this was a pivotal point in their relationship. Lucy spoke the truth about how many men—and most of society—viewed women. As she had, Sam had believed that he had a more enlightened view of the fairer sex, but the way he'd handled this situation made him wonder if he was more like his friends than he'd thought.

Putting himself in Lucy's place, he saw how his actions could be viewed as less than honorable. His motives might've been well-intentioned, but he'd handled things the wrong way. Lucy had a pleasant, witty disposition most of the time, but he was learning that there was an underlying, ironlike strength in her.

They were still newlyweds, still getting to know each other. He had to make a choice, the most important one in his life thus far. Did he want to spend the next several decades in a marriage marred by distrust and discord, or one blessed with love and happiness? Did he want to be less of a man than a woman like Lucy deserved, or did he want to be the man to whom she was proud to be wed? A man she could love and trust to keep not only her person safe, but also her heart?

His decision made, Sam rose from his chair and straightened his spine. "Lucy, from henceforth, I promise to never lie or go behind your back about anything again. Without trust and respect, a relationship, especially a marriage, cannot flourish. It will wither and die.

"I won't condemn either of us to that fate. Even if it angers you or hurts your feelings, I'll be completely honest about everything. No secrets, no dishonesty shall lie between us. This I vow to you now and forever more."

Lucy drew in a long breath and tears welled in her eyes. She didn't speak for long moments, but despite the torturous seconds that ticked by, Sam didn't rush her. Putting pressure on Lucy would be counterproductive, and most likely turn her from him.

As she searched his face, Sam tried to convey that his words were genuine, not a worthless promise.

At long last, Lucy started to smile. "I believe you, Sam." She tilted her head a bit as her smile turned teasing. "I'm going to hold you to that promise, too. We Irish take vows deathly serious."

Relief and happiness washed through Sam, making him grin. "As do I. Am I forgiven?"

Lucy sobered. "That depends."

"On what?"

"Whether ya help me clean up the kitchen or not."

Laughter burst forth from Sam and he reached her in three long strides. Sliding his arms around her waist, he held Lucy close and kissed her cheek. "If it'll keep me in your good graces, I'll wash dishes every night."

Lucy poked his chest and moved out of his arms. "Don't get carried away. I have a feeling I'll have to rewash more than a few."

Following her to the sink, Sam rolled up his sleeves. "I'll have you know that I'm no stranger to doing dishes, madam. I did them quite well when I was in the military."

Lucy let out a scoffing noise. "We'll see if a soldier can do dishes as good as me."

Sam stepped up to the sink and gave Lucy a smug smile. "Prepare to be amazed, Mrs. Slater."

# CHAPTER 13

*A* week later, shouts from outside startled Lucy and Sam awake. Lucy scrambled out of their bed and rushed to the window, Sam right behind her. Peering out, she gasped when she saw the unmistakable flicker of fire reflecting off the front of the barn.

Sam swore, snagged a pair of trousers from the back of the chair near his side of the bed, and shoved his legs into them. "I'll go see what's going on. Please go no further than the porch, Lucy. I'm not sure what we're dealing with yet."

Lucy wrapped a robe around herself while he put his boots on. "Aye. I'll put on some coffee and start pumping water into the big stew pots. No doubt it'll come in handy, either for fighting the fire or for you menfolk to clean up with."

Sam nodded and jogged through the house to the kitchen. Unlocking the door, he ran outside to find that the bunkhouse was on fire. He saw Grant filling buckets of water from the outside pump as fast as possible. Tom and Jensen ran them to Gray who threw the water on the flames.

Sam didn't waste time asking questions. There would be time for that later. Right now, they had to save the bunkhouse. He ran back into the kitchen, passing Lucy on the porch. Grabbing one of the big cast iron pots, he started cranking water into it. His strong muscles enabled him to pump fast and it was full in just a few pumps.

"Keep filling pots!" he shouted to Lucy as she entered the kitchen.

She nodded and rushed to the sink.

As fast as he could without sloshing water out of the pot, Sam hurried to the burning corner and threw the water at the base of the flames. A moment later, Gray did the same and it squelched some of the flames.

They fought the fire for the next twenty minutes before all the visible flames were out. They kept soaking the burned area for another fifteen minutes, to make sure that there were no smoldering embers inside that could reignite later. Finally satisfied, Gray called a halt to their efforts.

"Good work, everyone," he said. "We'll know a little better in the light of day, but I think the repairs will be minimal."

"I'm not worried about that," Sam said. "How did the fire start?"

Tom rubbed his stubbled chin, leaving a sooty smear behind. "I don't know. We were all asleep and the smell of smoke woke me up. I woke the other fellas, and when we ran out, we saw that the bunkhouse was on fire."

Jensen said, "I don't mind tellin' you, it gives me the heebie-jeebies thinking that we mighta burned up if Tom's nose hadn't worked so good."

Sam held up a lantern, inspecting the burned section. "I know that you men couldn't have caused the fire since you were sleeping, and it started on the outside. Someone lit this fire. Looks like they might have used alcohol or turpentine to get it started."

The other men looked it over and agreed with him. Lucy joined them, her brow puckered with worry. Sam told her their thoughts on the origin of the fire.

"So t'was arson, then," she responded with a shiver.

Sam put an arm around her. "Yes, but no one was harmed. We're all safe and sound."

Anger rose in him as he saw a tear escape the corner of her eye, leaving a trail as it slid down her face. Whoever was terrorizing them had to be stopped, but how could they do that when the culprits committed their crimes under the cover of darkness, when no one was about?

Stifling his fury, he kissed Lucy's forehead. Grant was there to guard Lucy during the day, so he couldn't stay up all night keeping watch. However, Sam didn't have the resources to hire another guard. Their budget was already strained.

"Why are they doing this to us?"

Lucy's question echoed Sam's thoughts.

"I know they want the land, but why? There must be other land they could buy. Why do they want this ranch so badly?" she asked.

"Mebbie there's gold or some sort of treasure buried on it," Jensen suggested.

Tom snorted. "I doubt that, so don't go getting any grand ideas about going on a treasure hunt, old man."

Jensen squared his shoulders. "Watch who you're callin' old, sonny boy. And it ain't that farfetched to think that someone buried something on the land way in the past and now someone's discovered it's here." His eyes bulged out. "Or it could be the Injuns. Mebbie there's an old grave site here and it's sacred to them."

"I don't think there's treasure on the land," Gray said. "But your notion about an Indian burial ground does have some merit. Perhaps you need to have another discussion with Drake, Sam."

Sam hated to think that Drake had held back on him about such a thing, but it could explain why they were going to such extreme measures to get rid of them. "All right. I guess it couldn't hurt. I'll ride out there tomorrow and see what he has to say."

"I think that's a good idea," Lucy said. "We have to get to the bottom of this. I wonder if Josh has had any leads?"

Gray said, "I must go to town tomorrow. I'll track him down and tell him what's happened."

Sam nodded. "Well, I guess there's nothing more to be done here. We might as well try to get a little shuteye."

"You all go to bed," Grant said. "I'm going to keep watch."

The other men offered to split the duty with him, but Grant refused. "There's no way I can go back to sleep tonight. No sense in anyone else losing sleep. Go on. I'll be fine."

As Sam walked back inside with Lucy, he thought about his impending visit to Drake in a few hours. He was fond of the young man, and it pained him to think that Drake might know who was responsible for all the problems at the ranch and hadn't told him. As much as Sam wanted the criminals caught, he hoped that Drake wasn't familiar with them.

THE ANGER SHINING in Drake's eyes as they sat at his campfire the next morning made Sam feel guilty for inquiring if anyone in his tribe might harbor any ill will towards him. Although he'd asked the question in the most diplomatic way possible, the implication was still the same.

Drake looked away from Sam, out over the flock of sheep. The sun was still low on the horizon, spreading golden light on the fields as it inched higher in the sky. His jaw clenched before he took a sip of coffee.

"I'm not trying to accuse anyone, Drake," Sam said.

Drake's gaze found Sam's again. "Aren't you? If I was a white man, would you be asking me this?"

His response echoed Lucy's question about whether he'd treat a man the same way he did a woman. It annoyed Sam to realize that in both cases, the answer would be no. The flaws of how society had shaped his worldview became glaringly obvious at that moment, and he didn't like it.

"I suppose not, but it's unlikely that a white shepherd who

worked for me would be trying to scare me off my land." Sam rubbed his forehead. "You have to look at it from my perspective, Drake. I have a wife to think of now. Lucy is new here and has no income of her own. It's a good thing that whoever shot at me was only trying to spook me, or else she'd return to being an unwed woman in a strange place. Her welfare is the most important thing to me."

Drake said, "I understand, but why do you think we might be involved?"

"I know that you have ancient burial ground around here. Are there any on my land?"

"No."

"Are you sure?"

"Yes."

Drake's firm tone reassured Sam that he was being truthful. Of course, he'd never known Drake or any of his family members to lie. Dishonesty was abhorred among the Crow and many other tribes.

If there were no sacred sites on his land, then no one in Drake's tribe had any reason to threaten him. Sam hadn't believed there was anyone within the Indian village who felt such animosity toward him, especially because he'd tended to many of their sick and had always been respectful towards them.

With a wry smile, he said, "I'll confess that I was half-hoping you knew someone who might be the guilty party. It would be one step closer to catching them and ending this."

"It's always easier to blame others who are different than you."

Sam cut a sharp glance at Drake. "That's not what I meant. I'm looking for clues anywhere I can find them. I just can't imagine anyone who has anything against me. Can you?"

Drake finished his coffee and sat his cup on the ground beside him. "No. I haven't heard anyone speak against you."

With a groan of frustration, Sam stood up. "Let me know if you do. I have a couple of patients to check on. Thank you for the coffee and for all your hard work. I'll bring your pay in a couple of days."

Drake grunted his agreement and Sam took his leave.

THE FOLLOWING EVENING, the church was packed with people. The previous day, Josh had announced that there would be a special town meeting, but he'd purposely omitted the reason it was being held. A lot more people were guaranteed to show up just to satisfy their curiosity.

A low hum of conversation filled the sanctuary as Josh walked to the altar and mounted the steps to the pulpit. He let out a piercing whistle that got everyone's attention, and the room quieted.

"Good evening, folks," he said with a friendly smile. "It's good to be here with you, but I wish it was for a different reason. As some of you know, I'm investigating ongoing crimes against our good doctor and his wife. So far, Sam's been shot at, someone has killed a bunch of their sheep, and threatened Mrs. Slater."

Murmurs of surprise and anger rippled through the crowd.

"And night before last, their bunkhouse was set on fire with four men inside it!"

The voices grew louder at Josh's startling announcement and he had to quiet them again.

"Now, I'm not gonna stand for good people being harassed like this. So, be warned, if the guilty party is in this room, I'm gonna catch you."

Everyone started looking around at each other in surprise. Josh took the opportunity to assess each person, searching for any traces of guilt in their expressions. However, what he found was shock and a little mistrust as the crowd conversed.

After a couple of minutes, Josh held up a hand. "All right. Quiet down, please."

Although a hush fell over the room, an air of disquiet remained.

"Now, I know that most of you around here are good, kind people, but there's someone among us who's trying to scare the Slaters off their land. Someone who's killed livestock and committed attempted murder twice," Josh said. "However, it's not just the Slaters who've had problems. The Crawford family has had some sheep slaughtered as well.

"Most of our fine citizens are ranchers and farmers, so this is an issue that affects a lot of us. If you have any information about these crimes, even if it's only a rumor, let me know and I'll follow up on it. All right. That's it for now. Thanks for coming out and have a pleasant evening."

Although an affable fellow, Josh was also astute and cunning. As the meeting broke up, he took note of who approached both of the families he'd mentioned to express concern and support. He watched the expressions and body language of the people who left right away for any signs of hostility against the Slaters or the Crawfords.

A few individuals stood out, but none that seemed overly suspicious. Although Josh was sociable with everyone who spoke to him, he observed them closely. However, none of them exhibited any odd behavior.

By the time he took his leave, Josh was convinced that unless they were excellent actors, the culprits weren't still present in the church. Disappointment weighed on him as he realized that he still had his work cut out for him, but he wouldn't give up until he'd caught the varmints.

# CHAPTER 14

*a*fter the fire, Lucy hadn't argued with Sam when he requested that she not leave the ranch alone. Thinking about how close the ranch workers had come to being gravely injured, or even killed, filled her with fright and anger. Knowing that Grant was always close by made her feel safe, and staying busy helped keep her mind off the scary incident.

So, Lucy finished making curtains for the parlor and both bedrooms. She scrubbed and polished all the floors, making them gleam, and she started making a wedding circle quilt for their bed. In the mornings after breakfast, she practiced her riding and was proud when the men complimented her on her progress. Feeding the men also kept her occupied. She baked bread and churned butter daily to have with the meals, and she made a couple of cakes.

But even with all this activity, Lucy was going stir-crazy

by the end of the week. She was in desperate need of some female company and wanted to catch up on what was happening in town. Friday morning, she completed her morning chores and made breakfast as usual. However, Grant wasn't present.

Sam informed her that he and Jensen had taken supplies and the week's pay out to the shepherds, but that they'd be back soon. As soon as Sam had departed for his office, and the other men went outside to resume their work, Lucy started cleaning up the kitchen. As she did so, she mentally went over her chore list for the day.

When she got to the third item, she realized that she'd forgotten to ask Sam to bring home yeast and corn starch the day before. There wasn't enough of either to make bread that day or to thicken the stew she'd intended to cook. Hopefully Grant would be back soon so she could go to town to pick some up.

When he didn't return by nine o'clock, she went in search of Tom or Gray, but found both of their horses gone. "They must be out moving the steer herd to another pasture or mending fences," she thought. She waited another half hour, but still no Grant or Jensen. Frustration grated on Lucy's nerves. If she didn't get her ingredients soon, she'd be forced to make something else for supper, and she didn't want to have to alter her plans for the day.

Lucy stood at the kitchen sink, drumming her fingers on the counter as she mulled over the situation. If she left now, she could make it to town and back with enough time left to carry out her original plan. But she'd promised Sam she wouldn't go alone.

Her fist clenched in anger at their tormentors. How long was this going to go on? What if it took months for Josh to bring in the criminals? Or what if he never caught them? She refused to live out the rest of her life in fear, hiding like a frightened mouse.

Her mind made up, Lucy retrieved her small money pouch and her derringer, and secured them inside her skirt pockets. On her way out, she snatched her hat from the row of pegs by the kitchen door and headed for the barn. Once she'd saddled one of their geldings, she mounted and put it into a fast trot.

Although she remained alert for any sign of danger, Lucy enjoyed the ride. A storm had rolled through the area last night, washing away any humidity. The cool, fresh breeze felt good against her cheeks and the air smelled of grass and flowers. Birds flitted back and forth in the trees, singing to each other.

Lucy's spirits lifted. "All right, Buck," she said to the horse. "Let's have a wee run, shall we?"

She urged the bay quarter horse gelding into a lope and laughed as the scenery sped by. Once she'd grown accustomed to the pace, she tapped her heels against Buck's side, sending him into a fast canter. The spunky horse snorted, enjoying the run as much as Lucy.

After a few minutes, Lucy pulled him back down to a trot and patted his neck. "What a nice lad ye are, Buck. Thanks for such a fun time."

Buck whickered low in his chest and bobbed his head a couple of times as if to say, "You're welcome."

As soon as she arrived in Spruce River, Lucy went to the mercantile, intent on getting her goods and returning home as quickly as possible. She'd inform Sam about her trip into town when he came home that night, but she didn't want to run into him while she was in town.

She greeted Mr. Frost, a large, middle-aged man with graying dark hair. He was a pleasant sort, and they were soon engaged in conversation for several minutes before she got on with her shopping.

"There you are!"

Lucy turned around at the sound of Jenny's voice, smiling at seeing her friend again. "Here I am."

Jenny linked arms with her. "Come have a cup of tea. I've been so busy that I haven't had the chance to come see you."

Lucy said, "I'd love to, but I'm in a bit of a hurry—"

Jenny tugged her in the direction of The Eatery. "We'll make it quick then. Just one cup."

"All right," Lucy agreed. "I'll finish my shopping and meet you in just a few minutes."

"Good. I'll get us a table," Jenny replied.

Wasting no time, Lucy picked up the remaining items she needed and put them in her saddlebags. She found Jenny sitting near the back of the restaurant, which suited her fine since it was away from the windows.

She'd no sooner sat down than Nell arrived at their table with a tea pot and teacups. She'd also brought a plate of assorted cookies. Lucy exchanged pleasantries with the wait-ress before Nell had to go serve other patrons.

As she poured their tea, Jenny asked, "Have there been any further incidents?"

"No, thankfully," Lucy replied. "I'm hoping that they'll give up since they can plainly see that we have no intentions of leaving. I'm not going to let anyone run me out of my home, and neither is Sam."

"I'm so glad to hear that." Jenny frowned. "I can't figure out what they want. Is it just the land itself?"

Lucy laughed. "I've been wondering the same thing. I thought maybe there was some sort of buried treasure around the place or something. I've spent a lot of time going over the house for any hidden compartments and looked around the property, too. But I didn't find anything."

"Well, it is valuable property," Jenny commented. "They must want it very badly to be going to such lengths."

"Aye, but they're not going to get it. Between Josh, Grant, and the other men, they'll be caught."

"You're right. Now, onto more pressing matters. Is married life still treating you well?" Jenny teased.

Lucy laughed and the two women started conversing about their respective husbands. Talking about something other than her troubles was a boon to Lucy and before she knew it, almost an hour had passed. After her third cup of tea, she announced that she had to leave.

"Well, thank you for such a nice time," Jenny said.

"Nay, thank you for the tea and conversation." Inspiration hit Lucy as she stood. "I'd like you and your family to come to

Sunday dinner this week. In fact, we'll make it a party. I think we can all do with a bit of fun."

Jenny's face lit up. "A splendid idea! I accept, and so will my family."

Lucy chuckled. "I have a feeling that they won't have a choice."

"Right you are."

Nell came to clear off their table.

"Nell, would you like to come to my party on Sunday?" Lucy asked.

Nell's mouth opened in shock and she almost dropped the teapot she'd just picked up. "Me, ma'am? Come to your party?"

"Yes. I'd love for you to come." Lucy touched Nell's arm. "Please say you will?"

Nell's face turned pink, but she offered her a shy smile and nodded. "I'd enjoy that very much."

"Good! Do you know where our ranch is?" Lucy asked.

"Yes," Nell said. "What time should I arrive?"

"How about two o'clock? That'll give people plenty of time after church," Lucy replied.

Jenny's eyebrows lifted. "People? How many are you inviting?"

Lucy said, "Well, I'd like to invite Pastor Paul and Annette, the Frosts, Greta Royal and Bill Eckert. I might decide on a few more, but that's it for now."

Giggling, Jenny said, "I wonder what Sam will say when you tell him."

Lucy lifted her chin. "I don't much care. I'm the lady of

the house and it's my right to throw parties, one of the few things that a woman doesn't seem to need a man's approval for. Ladies, it's been so good to see you. I really must be off. Thanks again for a nice time."

The other women bid her good day and Lucy walked back through the store. She found Damon stocking the candy near the front counter and invited him and Maggie to her party. That done, she hurried out to Buck, secured her full saddle-bags, and got underway.

As BUCK CARRIED her towards home, Lucy hummed and sang to her horse since they were the only ones on the road. Although she didn't have the most pleasant singing voice, she enjoyed it and Buck didn't seem to mind that she sometimes got off-key.

She kept the gelding at a trot most of the way because she needed to get home as soon as possible so she could get supper started. It would be a bit late as it was. She didn't feel bad about it, though. After all her hard work that week, she was due a little bit of fun.

Her mind turned towards the party and she wondered what she should wear. She couldn't wear one of her old dresses, and the event wouldn't be the kind to which one wore high fashion. Something in-between would be appropriate. Two of her dresses would suit, and she debated which one to choose.

She became so focused on planning the party that she didn't notice a rider approaching from the rear until the hoofbeats were quite close. Buck whickered a greeting to the other horse as Lucy turned in the saddle to see who it was.

A prickle of alarm spread over her shoulders when she saw a man with a blue bandana over his face closing in on her. She'd rarely seen men around town cover their faces, and since it had just rained last night, the road wasn't dusty enough to warrant wearing a bandana.

That combined with the cruel glint in the man's dark eyes turned Lucy's surprise to fear. She didn't bother greeting him, just tapped her heels to Buck's sides. He shifted into a lope, but the stranger was quicker in commanding his mount. The big chestnut rammed into Buck's shoulder, causing him to stumble.

Knocked off balance, Lucy grabbed the saddle horn to keep her seat, but she felt hands snag her shoulders. The next moment, she was yanked from the saddle. Her scream was cut short when she collided with the ground and hot pain shot through her right shoulder. She lay dazed, looking up at the sky.

She shrank back when the man came into view.

Menace gleamed in his eyes as he loomed over her. "You're coming with me. Don't scream or try any funny business if you want to live. Got it?"

Trying to remain calm, Lucy nodded. Her attacker grabbed her upper arms and hauled her to her feet. His actions hurt her throbbing shoulder, but she gritted her teeth against the pain.

He shoved her towards his horse. "Get on."

As she walked to the chestnut, Lucy remembered the gun hidden in her skirt pocket. Rubbing her shoulder, she moved her right hand down to the pocket and slipped it inside. Hope rose in her breast as her fingers curled around the small handle. Gripping it firmly, she gathered her courage and pulled it out, using her body to shield it from the thug's view.

She might not have enough brute strength to ward of her attacker, but she had a gun and surprise on her side. When the man's hand settled on her shoulder, she whirled around, aimed the gun at his stomach and pulled the trigger. He roared in pain as the bullet ripped through his abdomen.

Lucy screamed and shoved him away. He reached for her, but then clutched his stomach and fell to his knees. Nausea rolled through Lucy at the sight of blood seeping from between his fingers. Ignoring it, she thrust her weapon in her pocket and ran to Buck, who had stopped a short distance up the road.

As fast as her injured shoulder allowed, she pulled herself into the saddle and kicked Buck into motion. He caught her fear and lunged into a gallop. Lucy took gulping breaths to calm herself enough to guide the speeding horse.

The scenery flashed by, but Lucy didn't pay attention. She was intent on getting home and willed their lane to come into view. Tears of fright leaked from her eyes and were whisked away by the wind, created by their swift pace. With sheer determination, Lucy kept panic at bay. She glanced behind them a couple of times and was relieved to see that they weren't being pursued.

After what seemed like an eternity, their ranch came into view, and Lucy slowed Buck enough to make the turn without mishap. She urged Buck into a dead run again, riding him right up to the house where they skidded to a stop. Exhausted, Lucy could only sit on the gelding and try to catch her breath.

SAM ARRIVED home to an empty house. He'd finished with his patients and there were a few things around the ranch he'd wanted to get done that day. When he saw that Lucy wasn't in the kitchen, he searched the rest of the house, but didn't find her. He checked the garden, but there was no Lucy.

A sense of foreboding overtook him as he jogged to the barn. There was no one there, either. His unease grew when he saw that Buck's stall was empty.

"Lucy, you little fool," he muttered.

Intending to go after her, Sam was just exiting the barn to fetch Atlas from the paddock when Buck and Lucy raced past the barn. He watched the horse come to an abrupt halt, but Lucy made no move to dismount. Sam ran across the drive, reaching them in moments.

Buck stood with his head lowered, his lathered sides heaving from the heavy exertion. Lucy clung to the saddle horn, her forehead resting on her hands and her breath coming in gasps. He reached up and laid a hand on her arm, startled when she cried out and tried to hit him.

"Lucy, it's me! Sam."

"Oh, Sam!"

Lucy launched herself at him and her momentum almost knocked Sam down as she slid from the saddle and into his arms. She embraced him hard, squeezing him tight. Sam held her close as she trembled against him.

"Shh. It's all right now. You're safe, Lucy."

He kissed the top of her head, trying to comfort her by continuing to murmur soothing words and rub her back. It took a couple of minutes for her to calm down.

Drawing her away from him a little, Sam cupped her chin and made her look at him. "What happened, Lucy?"

The terror in her gray eyes tore at Sam. "I, there was a man, and we ran. I used my gun."

Sam's heart leapt. "You used your gun?"

She nodded vigorously, her ruined bun bobbing with the motion. "We were coming back from town. Me and Buck." She swallowed hard. "He attacked me. He was going to kidnap me." Her eyes squeezed shut tight. "I shot him in the stomach and got away."

Fear, anger, and relief sent Sam's blood pressure soaring and he couldn't speak right away. He cleared his throat and called on his doctor's detachment so he could find out exactly what had happened.

"Lucy, take a couple of deep breaths—"

Lucy pulled away from him and ran in the house. He followed her into the kitchen where she went straight to the cabinet and took down the bourbon decanter. "Lucy, now's not the time—"

"Oh, no, Sam. If ever there was a time, it's now!" She grabbed a tumbler and poured some of the alcohol into it. "I've never shot someone before." She took a gulp of the whiskey, grimaced and poured more.

Sam crossed the room and took the decanter from her. "I understand, but getting drunk won't help. Trust me." He pointed at the table. "Sit down here and gather your wits while I take care of Buck. Then you can tell me the full story."

He strode from the house, doing his best to control his emotions lest he scare Buck. Lucy's foolhardy actions weren't his fault. Sam patted the gelding's sweat-slick neck as he gathered the reins and turned him towards the barn. He kept the pace slow, giving Buck time to cool off a little, and himself time to calm down.

# CHAPTER 15

*L*ucy sat down at the table, but was right back up again, too full of nervous energy to remain still. She sipped her drink and paced around the kitchen, trying to come to grips with what had just happened. Was it real? She knew it was, but it was hard to believe. It was all so surreal.

She'd never thought she'd ever harm another human being, but she had. She tried to wall herself off from it, telling herself that she'd only acted to protect herself. But guilt slipped in through the cracks, filling her mind. Although her would-be kidnapper had put her life in danger, she had to know if he was all right.

Rushing from the house, she made it halfway to the barn before encountering Sam. She stopped in front of him and took his arm. "Sam, we have to go back to him. He needs help."

"Lucy, we're not going back there," Sam said. "Let's go back to the house and talk."

Lucy refused to move. "We have to. He's injured. You have to help him."

Sam's jaw clenched and anger filled his eyes. "I think the whisky has gone to your head. You're not thinking clearly. It's understandable after what happened."

Hot tears burned Lucy's eyes. "What if he died or he's dying? I might be a murderer!" She shook her head. "I can't live with that, Sam. Please!"

The sound of a galloping horse interrupted their conversation. They turned to see Grant coming in their direction. He rode up to them and dismounted.

"Lucy! There you are!" he said. "Are you all right? I was on the way home and found the signs of a struggle. There was blood on the road."

Lucy grabbed his arm. "Was he still there?"

"Was who there?" Grant asked, taking her hand.

"The man I shot. Did you see him?"

Grant's eyes widened. "You shot someone?"

"Let's all go to the house and talk about this," Sam said. "I don't know the full story yet."

The former soldier jerked his chin towards his horse. "I'll put Sully away and be right there."

Fuming because they wouldn't listen to her, Lucy started for the house, barely resisting the urge to stomp the whole way there.

Sam caught up with her. "I don't know why you're angry."

Lucy bit her cheek to keep from speaking. She just kept

walking with her eyes focused on their house. If he didn't understand her feelings, she wasn't going to spell it out for him when it was so obvious. His condescension was infuriating. Remaining silent was the best course of action, lest she say things she'd regret.

Sam put his hand on her shoulder, but she shrugged it off. Normally, she craved his touch, but she didn't welcome it right then. She was relieved when he didn't make a second attempt. Reaching the house, she went right to the stove, filled it with wood and got the fire going again. Then she put the kettle on.

"I have blood on me and I'm dirty. I'm going to clean up and change," she announced, and went to their bedroom.

Her right shoulder protested as she undressed. Looking at it in her dressing table mirror, she saw that a bruise had formed on the front of it. It was tender to the touch and the area was slightly swollen.

Sadness stole through her when she realized Sam hadn't asked if she was hurt. He was too angry and obstinate to bother, it seemed.

She put on a robe and went to the small washroom. Taking a bath would be wonderful, but it would have to wait. She washed off and combed out her hair, securing it with a ribbon. Going back to the bedroom, she decided to spare her shoulder and not bother wrestling with a corset. Instead, she put on a shift, a couple of petticoats, a camisole, and one of her thicker robes. It was a little warm, but comfortable.

Finished, she returned to the kitchen. By this time, Grant had arrived and was sat at the table with Sam. The kettle had just started to whistle.

"Would either of you like a cup of tea?" she asked, taking the kettle off the stove.

"Don't go to any trouble, Lucy. Seems like you've been through a terrible ordeal," Grant replied.

"'Tis no trouble. I'm making some for myself." She cut a glance at Sam. "I want to be clear-headed when I tell you my story."

Sam sighed. "I shouldn't have said that about the whiskey. I'm sorry, Lucy."

Lucy didn't respond as she fixed their drinks. Once she'd served them, she sat down and looked at the two men in turn. "I know that you're both angry with me for going into town on my own, but there was no one around to go with me. I waited until almost ten-thirty, but Grant and Jensen weren't back yet, and Tom and Gray weren't here, either."

Regret filled Grant's expression. "I'm sorry about that. It took us a little longer than expected because Jensen's horse threw a shoe and turned up lame. It was slow going to get him home."

"It's all right," Lucy said. "You didn't know that was going to happen."

"Why did you go to town?" Sam asked.

"I needed some cooking supplies I'd run out of," Lucy replied. "So, I saddled Buck and away we went. I went right to the store. I was just going to get my things and get right back home, but I ran into Jenny. It was so good to see her. We had a couple of cups of tea, and then I left."

Sam smiled. "I'm sure it was nice to see another female face after only having us men to talk to."

Lucy responded with a curt nod and took a sip of tea. "I left town, and I'd gotten about halfway home before it happened…" She took her time recounting the event, wanting to give as much detail as possible. It could be useful in catching the crook. "And so, we raced the rest of the way home. Buck has a lot of heart and he was so brave. Is he all right?"

"Yes. I cooled him off and rubbed him down. I gave him a little extra hay for all his hard work," Sam answered.

"Good. Thank you."

Grant stretched his legs out in front of him and crossed his arms over his chest. "It's my fault this happened. I shouldn't have gone this morning, but I wanted Jensen to show me where the herd is located right now. I should've checked to see if you needed to go to town, Lucy. I'm sorry."

Lucy shook her head. "I wouldn't have known right then. It wasn't until I went to make bread that I realized I was out of yeast and a few other things I needed. It's not your fault, Grant."

"That's kind of you, Lucy, but I promise that it won't happen again."

"Speaking of that, you can't guard me forever," she said. "We don't know if or when these scoundrels will be caught. I refuse to be a captive in my own home. I won't live my life always looking over my shoulder or afraid to be alone. I think I've proven that I can handle myself." She felt a twinge of nausea and took another sip of tea to calm her stomach. "Even though I feared for my life, I'm not proud that I shot a man. I'm glad that he was gone when you came through, Grant.

That means that he wasn't injured badly enough to prevent him from leaving, or that someone helped him."

Sam grunted. "Most likely one of his cronies. They're probably watching the ranch, but I'm also sure they're keeping watch in town. The guy you encountered must've followed you from there."

"Not necessarily," Grant countered. "They could also have a hiding place along the road into town. The woods provide great cover and it would be almost impossible to see someone hiding in a small thicket. We could've passed their hideout lots of times and never knew it."

A chill swept through Lucy at the thought of someone spying on her, just lying in wait for the chance to attack her. Her alarm must have shown on her face because Sam took her hand. Despite being upset with him, she didn't pull her hand from his comforting grasp.

He lifted her hand and pressed a kiss to her knuckles. "Darling, I know you're frightened, but we won't let anything else happen to you. And be assured that these men will be caught. Josh is working tirelessly, and he won't rest until they are. Neither will the rest of us."

Lucy pulled her hand from his and stood up. "Don't you see? I'm not the only one in danger. They almost killed Grant and the rest, and all of you ride around alone. You've already been shot at, Sam! We can't all ride around together in a posse or something."

Sam also rose. "I know that, but we can take every precaution possible until these thugs are apprehended. One of those precautions includes you not going to town on your own."

Lucy's hands clenched. "So, it's all right for you to go traipsing all over the countryside by yourself, but I can't even go into town? That's not fair, Sam. You didn't stay home or hire a bodyguard after you were shot at."

Sam's expression tightened. "It's different for me. I'm a doctor. I have patients to take care of and I'm the only one around here who can help them. It's a risk I have to take."

"I see." Lucy's nostrils flared. "You're a big, important man, so you get to defy these brutes and do as ye like. But poor, little me, a lowly housewife is forced to cower at home, like a good little wife should."

"That's not what I meant."

Discomfort spread over Grant's features. "I think I'll just give you two some privacy. Lucy, I won't be going anywhere tomorrow so I'll be at your disposal all day. I'm real proud of you, though, and I'm even happier that you're all right. Good night."

Lucy stopped him. "I'll be fixing supper in a bit. It'll just be something simple, but—"

"No, no. The boys and I can fend for ourselves tonight. You get some rest."

She barely resisted sighing as he went out the door.

"Lucy, now that he's gone, let me look at your shoulder."

Lucy's eyes flew to his. "How did you know?"

His lopsided smile made her heart flutter, even though she was angry. "There's not much I don't notice about you, sweetheart. I could tell from the way you were holding yourself that it hurt. You're also wearing a robe, which is easier to put on than a corset."

"Well, aren't you the smart one?" she snapped. "It's fine. I'll put some cold compresses on it and some liniment, and it'll be better in the morning."

"Please don't fight me on this," Sam said. "You could have a bone bruise or a slight fracture."

Knowing that he wasn't going to give up, Lucy stomped off to their room. She'd have to undress partway for him to examine her shoulder properly, so it wasn't a good idea to stay in the kitchen in case someone came to the door. Her mood wasn't improved by the fact that she was almost certain that she heard him chuckle as he followed her.

Once in their room, she undid her robe and took off her camisole. She untied the string at the neck of her shift that held it on her shoulders, and lowered the right side low enough to bare the joint. Looking up at Sam, she saw desire ignite in his eyes. With great effort, she ignored the sensual pull he had on her.

As his gaze lowered to her shoulder, Sam's expression grew concerned. With gentle hands, he examined her, apologizing each time she winced as he manipulated her arm.

When he finished, he drew her shift back over her shoulder and tied the string. "I don't think anything is broken, but the end of your collarbone near your shoulder is bruised and there are signs of a sprain. I'll draw you a hot bath to soak in. That and the liniment will help keep it from stiffening up too much overnight, but it's going to be very sore tomorrow."

Lucy groaned. "But I have so much to do!"

"You can do light chores to keep it flexible, but I'll take care of the milking and gather the eggs," Sam said. "Now, I'll go put water on to heat for your bath. Why don't you sit in your chair in the parlor, and I'll make you some willow bark tea to help with the pain."

How was she supposed to stay angry at him when he was being so kind? "Fine. I appreciate your help, but we're not done talking about this."

The amusement in his eyes made her angry again. "I didn't think for a moment that we were."

"Good." She put on her robe, turned on her heel, and left the room.

# CHAPTER 16

*P*ain lanced through Lucy's shoulder, waking her up. She groaned and opened her eyes. A throbbing burn filled her injured joint and she wished she could go back to sleep until it was healed. Sam had advised her against lying flat overnight, and she was glad that she'd listened to him. She could only imagine how much worse she'd feel if she hadn't.

"Good morning."

She moved her neck to the left in increments, testing to see how far she could turn it. It was a little sore, but she could stand it.

Sam sat on the edge of the bed, holding a breakfast tray. "It's not as good as your cooking, but I made you some breakfast."

A plate of scrambled eggs, bacon, and toast that was a little on the burnt side sat on the tray. There was also a cup of tea and a glass of milk.

Lucy's stomach gurgled, announcing that it was empty. "It looks wonderful."

Sam set the tray on the bureau and helped her sit up straighter. "I hope it tastes as good as it looks. Drink the tea first. It's willow bark for the pain."

She drained the teacup, anxious to feel better. Famished, she made quick work of the rest of her breakfast. When she finished, she relaxed back against the pillows, replete and content.

Sam took her hand. "Let me know how your pain is in a little while. I have some laudanum if you'd like it."

"I may take you up on that," Lucy said.

"As your doctor, I'm ordering you to rest today. There's nothing pressing that needs your attention, and we men can take care of your chores. Gray is going to cook supper, so everything is well in hand."

Although she hated not performing her duties, Lucy knew that she couldn't milk the cows or tend the garden. Gathering the eggs might also be tricky if the hens got cranky, which a few of them sometimes did. And washing clothes was completely out of the question.

She sighed. "Aye. Resting is best. I'll heal faster if I do."

"Right you are. That said, I don't want you to be bored. Would you like to read one of my books, or maybe work on your embroidery?"

Lucy thought about her options. "Reading would be fine. Choose for me. I'll also need my sketch pad and pencils. I could work on some designs. But I'd also like to talk to you about an idea I had for Sunday. I invited a few people out to the ranch for dinner Sunday afternoon in hopes of brightening up our spirits with a party."

Sam was a bit surprised that Lucy had invited people over to their home without first talking to him about it. But after everything they'd been through, a party didn't sound like a bad idea. After all, Lucy could probably use the company while she recovered. On the other hand, he wasn't sure if it was safe for people to come out to the ranch right now.

"When I go into town later today, I'll be sure to let everyone know whom you've invited to at least come out as a group," Sam reasoned. "I don't want to scare anyone, but they do deserve to know what's been going on." Lucy nodded her head, wondering if they should just cancel the party till things settled down at the ranch. But the more she thought about it, the more she reasoned that there was no reason to let these mysterious criminals win.

"I would appreciate that very much," Lucy replied as she looked up into Sam's eyes. "I have invited Jenny and her family, as well as Nell, Bill Eckert, and also the Reverend and his wife."

Sam smiled as he stood up. "Then I'll be sure to speak with them this afternoon. Alright, I'll go get the other items you need right away." He took the tray from her and left the room.

In a few minutes, he returned with the requested items and a cup of coffee. He set the drink on the nightstand beside her and put the other things on her lap.

Lucy smiled at his thoughtfulness. "Thank you. I need to take care of my morning business, though."

Unlike some men who would be embarrassed by her statement, Sam took it in his stride. "I should've thought of that. Sorry." He moved the things he'd just placed on her lap and drew the covers down. "Take your time and let me help you."

Lucy swung her legs off the bed and sat on the side. Other than a twinge, her shoulder didn't protest, but as she stood up, fire spread through the injured area, making her gasp. Sam was right there to steady her, and she was grateful for his support.

"Will you need help?" he asked, accompanying her down the hall to the washroom.

Lucy replied, "I think I can manage, but would you mind waiting in the hall in case I can't?"

"Of course, not. I'll do anything you need me to, Lucy."

She gave him a small smile and went into the washroom. Completing her toilet was somewhat difficult, but she gritted her teeth and got through it. However, by the time she opened the door, she was in agony.

"I'm ready for that laudanum now," she said.

"I thought that might be the case. I'm glad I didn't give it to you right away, though. It might have made you unsteady on your feet."

Sam helped her back to their room and resituated her in bed. She noticed a small medicine bottle and a spoon on the nightstand. Once she'd taken a dose, she washed the bitter liquid down with a couple sips of her coffee. Even though it was lukewarm now, it helped get rid of the awful taste.

"I'll be right at my desk working on a few charts if you need anything," Sam said.

Lucy chuckled. "You don't have to babysit me, Sam. I'll be all right if you have something else to go do."

"Actually, working on charts is exactly what I need to do. I'm a little behind, and keeping accurate records is important to me." A hint of mischief shone in his eyes. "But I will say that having you to look at from time to time will make the job quite pleasant."

Laughter bubbled up inside Lucy and she pressed a hand to her shoulder. "Don't make me laugh. Go on with ye, then. Do your work and leave me in peace."

Sam leaned down and pressed a kiss to her forehead. "As you wish. The medicine should be kicking in anytime now."

"Good. I'm all for it."

"I'm going to get some coffee. Would you like more?"

Lucy nodded and felt a little dizzy. The laudanum had begun to take effect. "No, thank you." She covered her mouth when she started to yawn. "I don't think I'll be awake for much longer. The medicine is quite powerful."

"Sleep then, sweetheart. I'll wake you for lunch."

Although she tried to respond to him, Lucy's eyelids were too heavy. Even before Sam exited the room, she'd drifted into slumber.

WHEN SUNDAY CAME, Lucy was feeling a little bit better. There was still lingering pain, but nothing like it had been a few days before. Planning this party had been the only thing that had really brought Lucy any joy lately. Her and Sam were still disagreeing from time to time, and despite what she said, she felt that Sam still didn't hear her. So, instead of arguing, Lucy had put her mind to making this party a success.

Sam had gone into town to attend services while Lucy stayed home to make sure all the food was ready by the time people started to show up after church. Lucy wasn't sure if she was ready to ride into town just yet, and though she regretted not being able to attend church, she figured some alone time from Sam would do her some good.

Lucy was pleased with herself for having baked a custard pie, along with several rolls with different flavors inside like peppered chicken, beef and tomatoes, and also mined meat. It reminded her of growing up within her Irish family and hoped to showcase some familiar dishes of her childhood now that she had the hang of cooking. Boiled potatoes and sauerkraut were amongst the other dishes, and by the time Lucy had set everything on the dining table, people were starting to arrive.

"Oh, Lucy, you look darling," Jenny Crawford said as she came into the house with her husband. "My goodness, doesn't it just smell lovely in here."

"Thank you, Jenny," Lucy said as they embraced carefully. Lucy was still trying to avoid bumping into anything with her sore shoulder.

"Sam told us what happened when you rode home the other day," Jenny continued. Lucy looked up to see Sam coming into the house with the Pastor Paul and his wife. They were chatting idly, so Lucy didn't try to interrupt them.

"Aye, it was quite an unfortunate event," Lucy agreed. "Come and fix yourselves something to eat." Lucy took the time to visit with all the guests as Nell and Bill Eckert came in as well. It was nice to talk to so many people when all she had to speak to was Sam and the cattle hands. It was good to be surrounded by other people, and also a few more women.

Even though they were in the same space, Lucy and Sam hardly said anything to one another. It appeared as though they were both trying to be on their best behavior in front of all their guests. But every time Lucy would laugh, Sam couldn't help but smile at his wife, thinking she had one of the most beautiful laughs in the world. And when Sam would start to describe something with much enthusiasm, Lucy was reminded how passionate Sam often was about his work and helping other people.

By the time the sun was setting, and everyone had enjoyed the dinner and conversation, along with Gray and the other ranch hands, the guests started to depart. Sam had wanted everyone to return to town before it got dark and insisted that they all travel together.

"Oh, come now, Dr. Slater. Don't be such a worry wort," Mr. Crawford said as he escorted his wife from the ranch home. The guests chuckled at the comment and Lucy felt justified in the way she felt in being kept at home. She raised her eyebrows at Sam but he didn't want to acknowledge her right now. Instead, he saw that everyone was settled before they departed.

When Sam entered the ranch house once more, Lucy was already busy doing the dishes. The house was empty save for the two of them and now Sam wondered what they were going to do. Thinking he best help his wife, Sam took dishes into the kitchen and started to help Lucy dry and put them away. As they worked together, neither one of them said a word. Lucy wanted the freedom to go where and when she pleased. And Sam was trying to do his best to hold his tongue so as not to upset her anymore. For now, he tried to at least be grateful that they'd had a pleasant evening together even if it had been by talking with other people.

THREE DAYS LATER, Sam and Lucy were on their way into town. The atmosphere between them was frosty at best. Sam's jaw ached from clenching it so hard to keep angry words at bay.

They'd argued about Lucy's desire for independence and were at a stalemate. Before he'd planned to leave that morning, Lucy had suggested that he take Grant along for protection. His hackles had risen over the implication that he needed it.

When he'd refused, she'd pressed him on why she had to be accompanied but he didn't, and their disagreement had escalated.

Lucy had then announced that since Sam was going to town, he could take her with him. She wanted to pick out some material and order some if the mercantile didn't stock it. She planned to stay in town to get to know people and drum up some business.

They'd agreed to meet at Sam's office at four o'clock and come home. Supper would be a simple affair since Lucy wouldn't get home in time to prepare a more involved meal by a reasonable hour.

Sam was relieved that her shoulder was feeling better, but that also meant she was returning to her more spirited self. Even though he was fuming on the inside, Sam kept an eye out for danger. Someone could be lurking anywhere —in the bushes, behind trees—there were so many places for unscrupulous characters to hide.

In a way, he was glad for the silence between him and his wife. He was able to listen to what was going on over the clip-clopping of their horse's hooves and the buggy wheels. Engaging in conversation would've reduced his level of concentration.

He glanced at Lucy. She sat staring straight ahead with a stubborn set to her jaw. Her hair was swept up into a high bun. Inky tendrils had escaped and fluttered against her pretty neck. Her cheeks were pink, no doubt because her temper was still running high.

Sam's hands tightened on the reins as he stifled the urge to kiss the nape of her neck and work his way around to capture her lips. Even though he was upset with her, his attraction to Lucy was even more powerful. Due to her shoulder injury, they hadn't made love in several days and he missed that close connection between them.

Holding back a sigh, Sam faced frontwards again and wondered how to resolve the situation.

"I know that I'm not supposed to be privy to our financial matters, but how much am I allowed to spend today?"

Sam frowned at her cool tone of voice. "I've never refused to divulge that information, Lucy. I'll be happy to go over the books with you. As for a spending limit, is fifteen dollars sufficient?"

Her head whipped around and her eyes met his for the first time since they'd left home. "That's far too much, Sam. I'll not spend more than ten at the most."

"All right. That's up to you. I just thought it would help you stock up on material in order to start your business."

A smile started to form on Lucy's mouth, but then she pursed her lips and looked away. "Don't think your generosity will placate me, Sam."

The frostiness had returned to her voice, which aggravated him. Why couldn't she see reason? Once again, he clenched his teeth to hold in the retort on the tip of his tongue.

"Why can't he understand my point of view?" Lucy lamented.

After a busy morning of shopping, she was ready for lunch. She'd decided to go to the Inn to catch up with Greta. The older woman had just sat down with her to eat her own meal.

"Men don't have to adhere to the same set of rules, so they don't understand our struggles, Lucy."

Lucy's cutting of her chicken grew more aggressive. "'Tis

the problem. The double standard makes me angry—no, makes me furious."

Greta eyed her. "That chicken is already dead. You don't have to kill it again."

Lucy smiled and softened her motions. "I'm sorry. It just vexes me sorely."

"I can tell. Sam isn't an unreasonable man. Surely you can work this out?"

Tears gathered in Lucy's eyes. "Aye, but not when it comes to this. I know he's trying to keep me safe, and I appreciate it to a certain point. I think that I proved that I can defend myself. What was the point of learning how to shoot if I have to cower and hide?"

Greta sipped her coffee for a few moments before responding. "Lucy, I've been around for a lot more years than you, and one thing I've learned is that men will usually not respond in a positive way to a woman who shouts or argues a lot."

Frustration gripped Lucy. "What am I supposed to do, then? Nod and smile and do whatever he says whether I want to or not?"

Greta raised her eyebrows. "I didn't say that. There are more effective ways of dealing with men and making them see things from your point of view."

"Not where I come from," Lucy said. "If Ma didn't yell and shout at Da, she would've never gotten her way about anything."

Greta reached over and patted her arm. "Well, there's no need for it to be like that between you and Sam. I believe you should be independent, but I have to agree with Sam somewhat. You shouldn't tempt fate just to prove a point."

Lucy wanted to stab the chicken with her fork. "And what happens if these igits are never caught? How long do I wait before I start moving about freely and living my life? As it is, Sam doesn't even want me walking out to the barn alone, but he and the other men can cavort around the ranch and all over God's creation all they like. Nice as it is, I refuse to be stuck in my house for the rest of my life!"

Greta glanced around the room. A couple of diners looked their way. "Please lower your voice."

Lucy blushed and looked down at her plate. "I'm sorry. I didn't mean to cause a scene. How do I get through to Sam? I tried this morning, but it was no use."

"I don't mean to pry, but how did you go about it?"

"I suggested that he should take Grant with him for safety." She couldn't hold back a smile. "He didn't like that at all."

Greta put her fingers to her mouth to muffle a laugh. "I'm not surprised. Men are prideful creatures and they like to think that they don't need protecting, that they're strong enough to deal with any enemy. Almost any man will get angry when his manhood is threatened, which is what you did."

Lucy finished her chicken. "I grew up with prideful men, so I understand. I was trying to show Sam how it feels to have someone suggest that you're not competent at something."

"Your reasoning is sound, but the way you went about it is where you went wrong."

Defeat weighed on Lucy, and her shoulders slumped. "I guess I might as well just accept that men will always be in

THE RECKLESS DOCTOR'S BRIDE

charge of women. I'll never be anything but a piece of property."

Greta reached across the table to squeeze her hand. "I know it's frustrating, but change takes time. I believe that someday women will be their own masters. We must help the cause along any way we can. However, certain methods are more effective than others."

Lucy managed a small smile. "I wish I shared your optimism. You said I went about it wrong. What should I do?"

"You have to show Sam that you're capable of protecting yourself. I know that you were successful against the man who attacked you, but that may not always be the case. Practice and become proficient with a weapon. Don't argue with Sam. When you become skilled enough, challenge him to a friendly competition and show him that you have no need for a body-guard any longer."

Hope rose in Lucy's heart as she thought about Greta's advice. The more she mulled it over, the clearer she saw the wisdom in her suggestion. "I think that's a splendid idea. That's exactly what I'll do. Thank you so much."

Greta patted her hand and stood up. "Happy to help. I must return to work now. I'll talk to you soon. I'm very curious to know how you make out."

"I promise to keep you up to date on my progress," Lucy said.

The two friends said goodbye.

As Lucy walked over to the mercantile, she decided on a course of action. Walking up to the counter, she greeted Damon.

"Back again, I see," he said.

Lucy smiled. "Aye. I need to purchase ammunition for a pistol and a rifle."

The surprise on Damon's face was comical. "You're buying ammunition? Is it for Sam?"

"Nay. It's for me."

Damon arched an eyebrow and seemed reluctant to give her the supplies. But when she fixed him with a hard stare and cocked her head a little, he started gathering the requested items.

"That'll bring your total today to thirteen dollars and ten cents."

Even with buying several bolts of material and the ammunition, she was still under the allotted spending limit Sam had given her.

"Thank you. Please put it on our account," she said. "We'll be by shortly after four o'clock to pay for everything and pick it up."

"Will do."

"Thank you, Mr. Frost. Ye've been very helpful today, and I appreciate it."

The big man grinned. "It was my pleasure. Always enjoy helping out a pretty lady."

Lucy laughed when he gave her a wink and left the store.

RIDING HOME THAT AFTERNOON, Sam was more confused than he could remember. Lucy's mood was the complete opposite from that morning. When she'd arrived at his office, she'd given him a peck on the cheek before he'd locked up. On the way to the store, she'd inquired about his day. They'd picked up her purchases and started for the ranch.

Now, she chatted about what a nice day she'd had and told him about having lunch with Greta. She'd also run into Pastor Paul, and they'd had a nice chat. While Sam was enjoying their conversation, he was baffled by her buoyant mood.

"When we get home, I'll make us some nice sausage, gravy, and biscuits. There's also the shoofly pie I made last night," Lucy commented.

"That sounds delicious. I'm starved. I'd be happy to help, if you like."

Lucy shook her head. "I'll be fine. It feels good to be up and moving about after being still for so long."

"I know what you mean, but please don't overdo it. I'd hate to see you relapse. Watching you be in so much pain was very difficult."

"I appreciate your concern. It's quite wonderful having my own personal doctor." The teasing smile she sent him made his blood run faster. "I think perhaps a thorough examination is in order later on. What do you think?"

"I think that could be arranged." Sam shook his head the next moment. "Am I talking to the same woman I came to town with this morning?"

Lucy's eyes sparkled as she laughed. "Aye. 'Tis."

"Are you sure? Because she was quite put out with me."

"I know, and I'm sorry. I just realized that there's no sense arguing about this anymore. All that matters is catching these thugs. I'll do my part by staying out of the way and heeding the advice of those who are experienced with this sort of thing."

Sam was still dubious. "Is this a trap of some kind? I find your quick capitulation a little suspicious."

"I promise that it's not a trick, Sam. It's just not important enough to keep fighting about," she replied with a shrug.

"That sounds more like resignation than agreement."

"'Tis neither," Lucy said. "It's acceptance of something I can't change right now. I have more important things to do than drive myself crazy over it. Such as starting my business." She slid over and tucked her hand in the crook of his arm. "I can't wait to start cutting patterns and making clothing."

It warmed Sam's heart to see her so excited. "I'll help in any way I can. Eventually, you might need your own shop in town. More women are coming West all the time. This area will become more populated before too long. People will need fashionable clothing."

Lucy rested her cheek against his shoulder. "I want to make affordable clothing. Anything from gowns and suits, to everyday clothes."

Sam kissed the top of her head and inhaled the scent of roses in her hair. She'd bathed last night, and she smelled wonderful. "You're wise to offer those kinds of products. They'll sell well. Both the town residents and travelers passing through will purchase them."

The rest of the ride home was spent discussing Lucy's plans for her future business venture. Sam was impressed with her business acumen and promotional ideas. He was fortunate to have married such an intelligent woman.

When they arrived at the ranch, Sam helped Lucy carry her purchases into the house, which they stored in the spare room. Then he went to take care of the wagon and horse while she started dinner. While he worked, he thought about the change in Lucy's attitude.

Her acceptance of the situation was a good thing, but it was obvious that she was still unhappy about it. However, he'd take her acceptance over obstinance any day. Once he was finished rubbing down their horse, he put it in its stall and headed for the house, looking forward to spending the evening with his beautiful wife.

# CHAPTER 17

*G*rant rubbed his jaw, indecision stamped on his face. "I don't know about this, Lucy."

"I already know how to shoot, but I need to improve. I'd also like to learn how to use a knife."

They stood in the kitchen. Everyone had gone for the day, leaving them alone.

"I don't like it," Grant said.

Lucy planted her hands on her hips. "If a man asked you to teach him to use weapons, would you?"

Grant's expression darkened. "That's not fair, Lucy."

"I disagree. It's very fair. I—" She broke off as Greta's advice echoed in her mind and she changed tactics. "Let's be honest. Josh is a highly skilled lawman from what I understand, but there's no guarantee that he'll find the people responsible.

"How long am I to be guarded? You're planning to leave

once you have enough money to buy a horse. What am I to do if these criminals haven't been caught by then? I must be able to defend myself."

Grant motioned for her to sit at the table and joined her. "Lucy, I won't leave until they've been apprehended."

"What if it takes six months, or even a year?" Lucy countered. "What if someone breaks into the house during the night while Sam is out on an emergency? You'll be out in the bunkhouse, and if I'm not able to scream, you won't know that I'm in trouble. What then?"

Grant frowned. "I see your logic. It's true that I can't be with you every minute of the day and night, but—"

"And what if someday when we have children, I need to protect them from something or someone?" Lucy had to work hard to keep her voice even. "Sam said this can be a harsh land filled with danger. He told me that women have to be more self-reliant than women back East because the men can't always be around. It's important for me to be proficient with weapons."

Grant looked out the window with a thoughtful expression on his face. Lucy didn't push for a response. It was wash day, so she took the large basket of dirty laundry outside and sat it by a huge metal tub.

Grabbing a pail, she went back inside and started pumping water into it. Grant still sat at the table, looking deep in thought. She let him alone and continued her work.

When the bucket was full, she started for the door with it. Grant rose and took the bucket from her, but he still didn't speak.

All through his assistance in readying the washtub, he remained silent. Right before Lucy started to wash the clothes, Grant finally spoke. "I'll teach you. You're right. I'll be leaving as soon as possible, and it will ease my conscience to know that you're well trained in defense and shooting."

Lucy wanted to jump up and shout her triumph to the sky, but she settled for beaming at Grant. "Thank you so much. This means more to me than I can truly tell you."

"You're welcome. I need to write a letter. I'll be right back. I can work on it while I sit here with you," he said.

"All right."

It turned out that Grant didn't get his letter written after all. He'd sat close by her and started it, but after the third time she'd stood up to hang an item on the nearby clothesline she'd strung between two trees in the yard across from the kitchen, he couldn't abide his inefficiency and started helping her.

Lucy washed and rinsed the clothes and he hung them on the line. The work went quicker, and they finished in good time. All the while, Grant had kept careful watch over his charge.

As she handed Grant the last shirt, she said, "Thank you for helping me. I have a little free time before lunch. How about a little lesson, and then I'll make us something nice to eat?"

Grant chuckled. "You sure don't waste time. Might as well."

Lucy stood up and started tugging one of the heavy tubs towards the side of the lawn where it was all right to dump it, but Grant jumped in to help again.

"Let me do this. These are heavy. It's easier for me to do it."

Proud though she was, Lucy's shoulder was still tender and lugging the heavy tubs would aggravate it. It already ached from using the washboard. "That's fine. I'll put these things away and be back with a gun and ammunition."

Grant pointed at the paddock. "I'll set up some targets there since none of the horses are out right now."

"Sounds like a good plan," Lucy said, and went on her way.

"That was some pretty shooting today, Miss Lucy."

Sam stopped chewing a bite of roasted chicken and looked at his wife.

"Thank you, Jensen, but I was only following Grant's instructions."

Grant speared a piece of potato with his fork. "Instruction will only get you so far. It's what a person does with new knowledge that matters. You paid attention and then put what I taught you into practice. You worked hard and did very well, so be proud of yourself."

Sam asked, "You've been target practicing today, Lucy?"

"Aye. In between my work I had some free time, so I asked Grant to teach me."

Although he looked a bit sheepish, Grant met Sam's gaze. "I thought we might as well put the time to good use, and it won't hurt for her to be able to shoot well."

Sam forced his voice to remain neutral. "I did give Lucy lessons, which is why she was able to fend off that lout who attacked her." That wasn't what he'd meant to say, but his tongue seemed to have a mind of its own.

"Right. The groundwork you laid with her really shows. You got her off to a solid start," Grant said.

Sam arched an eyebrow. "A solid start?"

"That's right. Lucy did well today, but there's still a lot I can teach her."

A note of challenge had entered Grant's voice and Sam didn't like it at all. "Such as?"

"She needs to be able to defend herself in close quarters in case her derringer would jam, or if her assailant would get the gun away from her," Grant replied.

Sam laid down his silverware. "She's not a soldier. She doesn't need that kind of training."

"She's also right in this room, lads." Irritation laced Lucy's words. "I'd appreciated it if you didn't talk about me as if I wasn't here."

"I'm sorry, Lucy. I didn't mean to be rude. I was just surprised," Sam said. "I thought we'd settled this yesterday."

"I was attacked and almost kidnapped." Lucy's hand tightened around her fork. "If I hadn't had that gun, God only knows what would've happened to me. I won't be a victim again, so with or without your permission, I'm going to learn how to better defend myself."

Anger burned in Sam's gut, not because of her assertive behavior, but because she wanted to learn from Grant instead of him. Jealousy was a foreign emotion for Sam, but the green-eyed monster was alive and well in his mind just then.

He chastised himself for his juvenile thoughts, but it was hard to quash them. Grant was an honorable man and more experienced in combat. While Sam had been treating injured soldiers, Grant had been out on the battlefield, right in the thick of the fighting. Sam's logical mind said that Grant was the better man for the job, but his pride was making it difficult to remain objective.

There was also the fact that Lucy had gone behind his back about this. She'd never mentioned that she was going to ask for Grant's assistance. Was this some sort of revenge for yesterday? Looking in Lucy's eyes, he detected no malice, but her expression was defiant.

Tom shifted in his seat and Sam became aware of the other men again. He was embarrassed enough and had no interest in having an audience witness an argument between him and Lucy.

He wiped his mouth and laid his napkin on the table. "I think this is a discussion best had in private, Lucy. If you'll all excuse me, I have some work to do."

Without another glance at his wife, he left the table and went to their room.

POUNDING on the kitchen door had Sam bolting up in bed. That kind of knocking almost always signaled something awful had occurred. He rushed from the room, jogging out to the kitchen. His gun sat on the table. He grabbed it and approached the door.

"Who is it?"

"Let us in, Sam."

Recognizing Gray's voice, Sam unlocked the door and admitted him into the kitchen. The fear in Gray's eyes set Sam's nerves on edge.

"Get your bag and come to the bunkhouse. It's Grant," Gray said.

"What happened?"

"We'll tell you out there. Hurry."

Sam turned around as Gray departed and almost ran Lucy over. He hadn't heard her come up behind him.

"What happened to Grant?" she asked, moving aside to allow him to pass.

Sam hurried down the hall to their room. "I don't know. Gray didn't say. Just told me to get my bag." He snatched it from where it sat on his desk. "Please start boiling water, Lucy. I have a feeling we're going to need it."

"Aye. Unfortunately, I think you're right." Lucy put a hand on his arm. "I'll help in whatever way I can, Sam. Just tell me what you want me to do."

Sam's smile was grim. "Thank you."

Calling on his ability to hold back his emotions during medical emergencies, Sam headed for the bunkhouse, preparing himself for the worst.

WHEN SHE TOOK HOT, wet towels and cloths to the bunkhouse, terror struck Lucy at the sight of Grant lying bloody and beaten on his bed. Sam and Gray had removed his shirt and blood oozed from two knife wounds: one in his right ribcage and one to the left side of his abdomen. Both looked deep and lethal. Lucy felt a little woozy at first, but she rallied, refusing to faint over some blood and let Grant and Sam down.

Lucy walked over to a square wooden table in the middle of the bunkhouse. The men's beds were set up in a horseshoe pattern, with Grant's being the one to the left of the door.

"Everything is here, Sam," she said. "Jensen, will you please light your campfire?"

The older man's face had turned ashen and Lucy thought that some fresh air would do him good. They didn't need him passing out on them.

"Sure thing," Jensen said, looking relieved to get out of there. He wasted no time leaving.

"What happened?" Sam asked, as he gave Grant a large dose of laudanum. The former soldier was barely able to swallow it.

Gray replied, "We went to Handy's. Tom and I became engaged in a game of poker. Grant went to do the necessary out back of the saloon. The next thing we knew, he came staggering in the door and collapsed. From what we could gather, three men attacked him and left him to die."

Lucy's burning anger was mirrored on Sam's face. "They have to be involved in what's going on around here. Hopefully he'll be able to tell us who they were when he wakes up."

Tom sat down on his bunk. "If I find out who they are, I'll kill them."

Gray rested a hand on his shoulder. "No, you won't. The guilty parties will face justice, but not at the hands of vigilantes. Understand?"

Tom looked like he was going to argue for a moment, but then nodded.

Lucy was glad. There had been enough violence and bloodshed. It had to end somewhere. She moved closer to Grant, forcing herself to watch what Sam was doing. She had to become accustomed to this sort of thing. No doubt she'd witness many medical emergencies in the coming years.

"How can I help?" she asked.

"Can you keep pressure on his stomach while I work on the rib puncture?"

"Aye."

Lucy took over for Sam, and he moved over to further examine the other wound. Grant let out a weak moan when she pressed a fresh towel against his abdomen. She blinked back tears at the thought of causing Grant pain, but she knew what she was doing was important, and that it could save his life.

"I don't believe this stab hit anything vital," Sam said. "It doesn't seem like the lung has been punctured. I'm going to cauterize the wound to stop the bleeding."

Gray opened Sam's bag. "I'll heat your knife."

Lucy blanched at the idea but didn't let up on her test. Gray took the knife outside to heat in the flames of the fire

Jensen had started. Several minutes later he returned with it. The blade glowed red-hot.

Sam poured whiskey onto a clean cloth and wiped the injured area with it. "Lucy, keep up that pressure. Gentlemen, hold him down and keep him as still as possible. I'll make this as quick as I can."

The men moved into position and Lucy steeled herself for what was coming.

Gray put a leather strap between Grant's teeth. "Bite down, lad."

Despite his glazed over eyes, Grant heard Gray and gave a slight nod.

Sam's eyes moved between those gathered around the bed. "Here we go."

Sam pressed the knife blade across the wound. Grant stiffened and let out a muffled cry as the scent of burnt flesh filled the bunkhouse.

Lucy closed her eyes against the nausea that churned in her stomach. Grant writhed under her hands, and she followed his movements, keeping the pressure on his stomach steady. She opened her eyes when Grant relaxed and fell silent. "What happened?"

"He passed out," Tom said.

Sam started bandaging the burn site. "It's a blessing. He's going to be in a lot more pain before we're through. That stomach wound is going to be much more difficult to deal with."

Sympathy flooded Lucy, strengthening her resolve to help

in any way possible. Grant had been good to her and she considered him a friend.

Sam moved closer and smiled at Lucy. "Let's see how this is doing."

Lucy cautiously removed the towel, which was almost soaked with blood. More started flowing from the wound at an alarming rate as soon as she took the towel away.

"His artery has been damaged. I need to repair it," Sam said.

Lucy's heart hammered in her chest. "Can you do it here?"

Sam replied, "I've repaired far worse and in far worse places. But I have to be quick and I might need your sewing skills. Do you think you can help?"

Fear clogged Lucy's throat, making her reply almost a whisper. "You want me to help perform surgery?"

The intense way Sam stared into her eyes scared her even more because it indicated that he was dead serious. "If need be, yes. I hate to pressure you, but time is of the essence. Can you help me?"

"You did a beautiful job with all the curtains, Miss Lucy. I reckon you could help the doc patch Grant up just as good," Tom said with a wink.

Lucy was about to berate him for making light of the situation, but Sam's chuckle stopped her.

"You might even make him a little prettier," Gray chimed in.

The right corner of her mouth quirked up as she caught on. Using humor to deal with difficult situations wasn't a strange concept to Lucy. Looking down at Grant lying so still on the bed, his hair soaked with sweat, she knew that refusing wasn't an option.

"Aye. I'll help. Just tell me what to do."

"Good. Let's begin."

Though Sam's statement was curt, the pride shining in his eyes bespoke his admiration and approval of her. She wondered how he could be proud of her for one form a bravery but not for another. Knowing this was no time for such thoughts, she locked them in a mental box and began following Sam's instructions.

THE SURGERY WAS a harrowing ordeal despite the short time it took. While he'd been unconscious, they'd moved Grant onto a makeshift operating table made from long wooden boards laid over wooden sawhorses. Lucy had covered the boards with two old horse blankets for cushioning.

Several lanterns were hung around the table to give them as much light as possible. Sam instructed Gray on how to administer chloroform to Grant. He'd ordered the expensive anesthetic several months ago and was now glad that he had. It meant that Grant wouldn't be subjected to the agony of an invasive surgery while being completely aware of what was occurring.

Sam monitored Grant and waited to make an incision until he was certain that he was fully under. When Grant remained motionless, save for his breathing, Sam went to work. Although he wished that he had an operating theater with all the new medical equipment available, Sam was used to performing surgery in difficult circumstances. Compared to treating wounded soldiers on the battlefield, performing an operation in a bunkhouse was a luxury.

Although Sam had an excellent education and was a skilled surgeon, he felt a little inadequate. There were new procedures he didn't know about, and he worried that he wasn't up to par for what Grant needed done. Abdominal surgery was a tricky business even in the best conditions, let alone their current one.

Lucy's gasp as blood gushed from the new incision almost made him glance at her. "Lucy, I know this is all shocking to you, but please don't make sudden noises or bump me. It wouldn't take much for me to nick something vital."

"I'm so sorry." Lucy's words were heavy with regret. "I'll be very careful, Sam."

"Thank you."

Sam instructed Lucy to soak up blood with clean linen cloths while he worked. His excellent grasp of anatomy enabled him to find the two damaged blood vessels. He repaired the first one without much difficulty, but the second one was difficult to reach, since he had large hands.

He glanced at Lucy, relieved to see that although her face was pale, she was avidly watching him. "Lucy, do you see this vein that's been cut?"

She leaned closer and nodded after a moment. "Aye."

He moved his index finger a fraction. "This is the other part of it. Do you think you can sew them together?"

Her mouth dropped open as she gaped at him. "I've never

done anything like that. What if I do it wrong and kill him? I couldn't bear it."

Sam smiled reassuringly. "I felt the same way the first time I operated on someone. It wasn't easy but knowing the patient would certainly die if I didn't at least try motivated me.

"You have smaller hands than me, Lucy. If we can't get this bleeding stopped, Grant will die. I'll guide you the entire time. Will you try for his sake?"

The fearful expression on her face made Sam afraid that she was going to refuse, but then she squared her shoulders and pulled herself together. "I'll do my best. Don't let me kill him, all right?"

Her determination and use of humor made Sam even more proud of her. "I'll do my utmost to not let that happen."

At her brisk nod, Sam began instructing Lucy. He was impressed by her deft handling of the needle and thread. If her sutures were a bit clumsy, it was only because she was nervous, not because she wasn't capable.

With more practice, Sam felt confident that she could out-suture many surgeons. When she'd successfully tied off the vein, he couldn't resist kissing her cheek. "Well done, my love. I'll take over now. It's imperative that we get him closed up now."

Lucy turned white and he knew what would happen next. She nodded and fled from the bunkhouse. The sound of retching reached him as he worked, but he couldn't stop to go check on her. Her reaction was completely understandable. To be thrown into major surgery without any prior medical experience was beyond daunting, but Lucy had borne up well under the strain.

Before long, he finished closing and stepped back from his patient. "You can stop with the chloroform now, Gray."

Gray took the handkerchief away from Grant's face and sat the bottle of anesthetic on the table. It was almost gone. "Looks like you finished in the nick of time."

Sam sighed as he started washing and rinsing his hands and forearms in the large basins of hot water. Lucy had returned at some point, prepared the basins and started cleaning up the area.

Looking over, he saw her changing Grant's bed and felt a rush of intense emotion roll through him as he watched her. Love so powerful, so raw, suffused his heart and he could hardly restrain himself from blurting it out. It wasn't at all the right time, so he kept it locked inside. But at the earliest possible time, he would tell his stunning wife that he'd fallen in love with her.

LUCY HAD BEEN FREQUENTLY BATHING Grant, trying to cool him off. He'd woken a couple of times, but Sam had given him more laudanum, so he'd remained asleep most of the time.

She agreed with Sam's strategy. If Grant rested, he would heal faster because he wasn't moving around, putting pressure on his injured areas. Sam was confident that Grant would make a full recovery from his wounds, but the infection posed a dire threat to him.

Her eyes were gritty from exhaustion, but Lucy refused to leave Grant's side. She felt a deep responsibility to him. Having her hands inside his body had created an intimate connection to him, and she was scared that her participation in the surgery had been inferior and that he would perish as a result. Sam had assured her several times that she'd done a splendid job, but she was still doubtful.

Drawing the covers down until Grant's torso was revealed. Lucy carefully bathed his shoulders and arms, making sure to avoid his bandaged midsection.

Just as she finished, Sam came in. "How's he doing?"

Lucy sighed. "His fever has not broken. Isn't there something more we can do?"

Sam held up a jar. "Actually, there is. I had Tom ride out to Drake's village to visit their medicine woman. The Crow have many remedies that white people don't. This poultice is to be spread on his feet and his feet should be wrapped up. They use it to reduce fever and drive out infection. I also made a tincture of honey for him to drink, which is very good for healing and helps to relieve inflammation. Once his pain level starts to decrease, we can switch to willow bark tea. I don't like to keep patients on laudanum any longer than necessary because it's addictive."

"I'll put the poultice on," Lucy said, starting to rise. She swayed on her feet a little.

"No, you won't. You need to sleep," Sam said. "You're no good to Grant if you collapse. You also need to eat."

"I'm fine," she insisted.

Sam put an arm around her shoulders and guided her towards the door. "No, you're not. I'm going to get you something to eat and then you're going to bed."

Lucy didn't have the strength to argue. She let Sam take her to the house where he fixed her eggs and bacon. Until she took the first bite, she didn't realize that she was so famished. Her breakfast disappeared in a flash and she washed it down with the cup of tea Sam made her.

A huge yawn gripped her as she rose from the table. She went to their room, stripped down to her shift and fell into bed. She fell asleep so fast that she never remembered Sam pulling the covers over her.

## CHAPTER 18

*R*iding up to the Slaters' house, Josh dismounted and tied his horse to the hitching post there. Gray had tracked him down at the Inn to let him know that Grant was awake, so he'd come right away. He hoped that Grant could give him some information about his attackers.

Although he'd gotten a few leads, none of them had panned out so far. As he walked towards the bunkhouse, Lucy came out.

"Morning, Josh."

Josh removed his hat. "Morning, Miss Lucy. How are you?"

The fatigue in her face couldn't quite be erased by her smile, but she was still beautiful. *Sam's a lucky man,* Josh thought.

"I'm fine, thanks, and you?"

He nodded towards the bunkhouse. "I'll be better if Grant

has some useful information for me. I want to catch these ba—um, dirtbags," he amended. Although he was frustrated, he remembered his manners at the last moment.

Lucy's eyebrows drew together. "I hope he does, too, but he's still weak so please don't tire him out more than necessary."

"I'll keep it as brief as possible," Josh promised. "How is he?"

"Better now that the infection is subsiding, but he still has a long recovery ahead."

"Well, he's a strong fella, and he's got the best people looking after him. I'm sure he'll be back to his old self in no time," Josh responded.

Lucy smiled. "I hope so. I pray that he doesn't have any setbacks."

"Same here," Josh agreed. "Well, how's about I get on with it so he can go back to resting?"

"Aye. That would be good."

Josh followed her into the bunkhouse and looked around, noticing that it looked a little nicer than the last time he'd been there. Dark blue curtains hung at the windows and a new braided rug covered the floor in the middle of the room. Everything looked clean and tidy.

"Lucy insisted that the place needed some sprucing up."

Josh turned at the sound of Grant's voice. He sat in bed, propped up by several pillows. He looked haggard and pale, but his eyes were clear and he was lucid—all good signs.

"I'd say she was right." Josh took a chair from the table,

moved it over to Grant's bunk and sat it down by it. "Certainly does look nicer in here."

Grant shifted his position a little. "Agreed."

Josh sat down. "What do you remember about the attack? Don't leave anything out. Even the tiniest detail might be important."

"I've had a lot of time to think about it, and most of it is very clear to me," Grant said. "I went with Gray and Tom to Handy's. They got into a poker game, but I didn't join in since I'm saving up money. I watched for a little while and then went to the outhouse.

"When I came out, three men approached me. I knew they were up to no good just from the way they moved. I backed up against the outhouse to protect my back and drew my pistol. I gave them every opportunity to back out, but they wouldn't."

Josh leaned forward in his chair a little. "Did you recognize any of them?"

Grant shook his head. "No. It was dark and I'm still new around here. But I did see the guy's face who did this to me, and I can identify him."

Excitement flooded Josh, but he kept a level head as he pulled a small notepad and pencil stub from his shirt pocket. "Please describe him to me."

Grant obliged, telling Josh every detail he could remember. "While we were struggling, I noticed that he had a scar that ran from the left corner of his upper lip almost to his nose."

That made Josh sit up a little straighter. "Are you sure about that?"

Grant grimaced as he shifted in bed a little. "Positive. Why? Does that mean something to you?"

"Based on that last tidbit and the rest of your description, I'm positive that I know who the guy is," Josh replied.

"Who?" Grant asked.

"The brother of a fella I hauled off to prison several months ago. Andy Franklin was abusing his wife and kids. He's locked up in Helena now," Josh said. "The Franklins have always been jealous of Mason Crawford's family because their land is so fertile. The Franklins' place is mainly rocky soil that doesn't yield many crops."

Lucy asked, "Do you think it's the Franklins who've been threatening us?"

"I think it's a real possibility. Your land is just as good quality as Mason's." Josh stood up. "Looks like I'll be taking a ride out to their place to have a talk with them. I didn't know that any of the other Franklins were around since Andy's wife took the kids and moved back East." He held out a hand to Grant. "I'm real glad to see that you're on the mend. Thanks for all the information."

Grant shook his hand. "Happy to help. Let us know what happens."

"I sure will."

Lucy followed Josh out to his horse. "Why do you think those men attacked Grant? It's me and Sam that they're after."

As he unwound his horse's reins from the hitching post, Josh considered his words carefully. He didn't want to scare Lucy, but he felt that she deserved his honesty. "They went after Grant for a couple of reasons. Hurting or killing Grant might drive you folks to get off this land, but if it didn't, at least he wouldn't be around to get in their way."

Lucy's eyes widened, but she didn't look away. "What you mean is that he wouldn't be here to protect me anymore."

"That's right. So, until I bring these guys in, be extra careful," Josh responded. "They're getting more desperate, so there's no telling what they'll try next. Understand?"

A fierce light lit her eyes. "Aye. I understand and I'll be prepared if anyone tries something."

"Lucy, don't go looking for trouble," Josh said. "I don't want you or anyone else getting hurt."

"I won't go looking for it, but if someone brings trouble to us, I won't run from it," Lucy told him. "This is our land, our home, and I'll be darned if anyone is going to run us off. Be careful, Josh."

"Yes, ma'am, and you do the same."

She gave him a curt nod and headed back to the bunkhouse. Josh watched her go for a moment before mounting up. As he trotted his horse to the main road, Josh admired Lucy's bravery, but he hoped she'd heed his warning. The Franklins were not people to trifle with.

SAM KEPT Atlas at a lope the whole way home from Mrs. Stavros's ranch. He'd been checking on her granddaughter, Elise, who'd broken her arm last week. The rambunctious six-year-old had been playing with her older brother near the creek. They'd been skipping rocks and had tussled over a very nice, smooth specimen.

Their two mongrel dogs hadn't liked their arguing and had tried to break it up. When they jumped on the kids, all four of them had tumbled into the shallow creek. Poor Elise had tried to break her fall and had broken one of the bones in her forearm in the process.

Once he'd ascertained that Elise was coming along well, he'd said his farewells and went on his way. He wasn't far from his ranch when he heard gunshots in the distance. They were relatively close, which made his heart lurch in fear. Was someone attacking his ranch?

His alarm abated somewhat when he realized that the shooting was coming from a different direction. He listened for a moment and knew that this wasn't someone doing some target practice. Somewhere to his right, a gunfight was in progress.

Sam looked in the direction of home for several moments. Although he wanted to get home to his wife, he couldn't ignore the fact that someone might need his help. With a click to Atlas, he put the big horse in motion, speeding towards the unknown danger.

FOLLOWING THE GUNFIRE, Sam was surprised that it led to the Franklin ranch. He'd been told that it had been empty since Andy's wife and children had moved away. If that was the case, who was having a shootout there?

Sam brought Atlas to a halt at a thin stand of trees before the place and proceeded on foot from there. With great caution, he approached the faded, graying barn that had seen better days. He made it to the back of it and cringed when he heard at least two guns fire.

The sound had come from the direction of the house. Sam chanced a peek around the corner of the barn and saw Eddie Murtaugh hiding behind the stone well that stood between the house and barn. A bullet ricocheted off the well, making Eddie jerk.

Swinging his gaze to the right, Sam saw Eddie's brother Sawyer standing behind a big oak tree, aiming his rifle at the house. He fired and the bullet shattered a glass pane of one of the front windows.

Eddie and Sawyer Murtaugh often acted as deputies for Josh, and Sam surmised that they were doing so now. But who were they after? Had they chased some criminal here, who was now holed up here?

Sam examined the area before creeping along the side of the barn towards Eddie's hiding place. Eddie saw Sam and grinned. The Murtaugh brothers were known for their bravery, cunning, and for liking fights a little too much. Staying low, Sam ran over to another tree that stood near Eddie.

"What's going on?" he asked between gunshots.

Eddie said, "We've got Titus, Art, and maybe Zeb Franklin pinned down in there."

Sam arched an eyebrow. "Why? What did they do?"

"Josh is pretty sure that they're the ones who've been after you and yours," Eddie replied. "Turns out that Grant recognized the guy who stabbed him, and he fits Titus's description. Josh just wanted to talk to them, but as soon as we got here, they started shooting at us."

Rage built inside Sam until the landscape took on a red tinge. He gripped the handle of his revolver as he contemplated blasting his way into the house. The next moment, he rejected that idea. He needed more information before charging into the situation like a bull in a china shop. Doing that could get him killed. His thirst for revenge would have to wait to be quenched, since he had no intention of making Lucy a widow.

"Where's Josh?" Sam asked.

"He's over there by that old wagon."

Sam looked where he pointed and saw his friend hunkered down behind the rickety structure. Josh shouted for the occupants of the house to lay down their weapons and come out. He was answered by a volley of shots.

When it subsided, Sam sprinted to Josh's position, cringing when a bullet hit the ground two feet away from him. Gaining the safety of the wagon, he crouched by Josh and smiled. "Looks like you're all having fun."

Josh grunted. "What are you doing here?"

"I was on my way home and heard all the shooting. Eddie says you have the suspect of Grant's attack holed up in there."

"That's right. I'd bet my last penny that Titus Franklin is behind all this. I don't put anything past that polecat," Josh said. "There are a couple of other guys with him, but I'm not sure who they are. I recognized Titus's voice, though. I didn't know he'd come back to town, but I guess he did."

Sam had to clamp down on his anger again. "So, they're the ones who've be after us. What's your plan?"

"Well, just like you do with rats, I'm gonna smoke them out. Robert Red Dog is out back, putting that part into motion."

Shortly after Josh spoke, the sound of breaking glass reached them, followed by a lot of shouting. The two men raised their heads just high enough above the wagon to be able to see the ramshackle white house. Smoke started coming out of one of the front windows and the yelling turned into coughing.

The front door opened, and four men rushed from the house, guns blazing as they made a break for the barn.

"I hope you're a good shot, Sam," Josh commented. "We could use you."

The thought of aiding in the apprehension of the men who'd terrorized his wife and almost murdered Grant filled Sam with satisfaction. He cocked his gun. "It'll be my pleasure to help bring these goons to justice."

"Glad to hear it. Let's go."

Josh stood up and shouted, "Titus! You and your men surrender now, and no one has to get hurt!" One of the thugs shot at Josh, who ducked. "I'll take that as a no. All right. I guess we're going to do this the hard way."

Things got even crazier and bullets were exchanged with dizzying speed. Sam joined in the fray and didn't feel bad when he shot one of the guys in the leg. The man lay screaming until another gunshot hit him in the chest, forever silencing him. Sam had been taught to save lives, not take them, but he felt no sadness that the man was dead.

Somewhere to his and Josh's right a man screamed.

"I don't see Sawyer anywhere," Josh said. "I'll bet he got that fella. Time to get the rest."

Josh left their hiding place, running towards the barn. As Sam followed him, he saw a man step out from behind a bush. He acted before he truly registered his actions. Sam raised his gun, took quick aim and fired. His shot connected with the guy, who twisted to the left from the force of the bullet's impact and crumpled to the ground.

Several other shots echoed off the buildings before everything went quiet.

"Eddie! Sawyer!" Josh shouted as he approached the criminal Sam had shot. "Are you fellas all right?"

"We're fine!" Sawyer called back as he joined Josh and Sam. "Can't say the same for these sidewinders, though."

Sam walked over to his victim and looked down at him. An ugly scar marred the man's features. "Is this Titus?"

"Yep. That's him," Josh answered. "Looks like you spared me having to make a trip to Helena, Sam."

Sam holstered his weapon and crouched next to Titus, making sure he was dead. "You're right. He's gone."

All the others had also been killed.

Josh congratulated his deputies on their excellent work, and they moved the deceased into the barn. The sheriff said he'd have the undertaker come out for them as soon as he got to town.

"I'll bet it feels good to know that you guys are safe now, Sam," Josh said.

Sam smiled. "Thanks to you."

Josh shook his head. "No, it wasn't just me. If it wasn't for Grant's description, I'd still be scratching my head. Well, why don't you get home to that wife of yours and I'll finish up here."

Sam didn't argue with Josh about it. He thanked him and the Murtaugh's again, mounted Atlas and urged the gelding into a canter. He couldn't wait to tell Lucy that their nightmare was over. He also couldn't wait to tell her how he felt about her. With a smile on his face, he sent Atlas galloping for home.

As THEY STOOD in the kitchen, Lucy listened to Sam's story with a mixture of relief, fear, and anger. She was happy that no one else would be hurt and that she didn't have to constantly be on the alert any longer, but the way Sam had placed himself in danger made her furious.

"So, it's over," he said, resting his hands on her shoulders. "No more danger, or reason to live in fear. Everything is fine now."

Lucy pulled away from him. "Fine! You think everything is fine now?"

The confusion in Sam's expression only made her angrier. "Yes. The threat is past. Why are you so upset?"

Lucy held back angry tears. "You berated me for having

the audacity to want to protect myself by learning how to shoot better, but it's perfectly all right for you to go rushing into a gunfight! You could've been killed, Sam!"

"Lucy, it's not the same thing at all," he said.

"Why, Sam? Explain why it isn't?"

Sam put his hands on his hips. "Because I'm a former soldier and I've fought in battles. You haven't."

"I may not have fought in a war, but I've fought a battle!" Lucy shouted. "How could you go do something like this? What would I have done if…?" She couldn't finish. Her vision blurred from the tears she could no longer keep at bay, and she realized that she was no longer angry with Sam because of their ongoing disagreement. No, she was enraged with him for a much different reason.

"Lucy, I'm fine. Not a scratch on me. Calm down, sweetheart," he said.

"Don't tell me to calm down like I'm some child, Sam." She pointed towards the bunkhouse. "There's a man lying inside there who almost died several days ago—a seasoned soldier, mind you. If that can happen to him, it could've happened to you. Losing Grant would be terrible, but if something happened to you, it would be so much worse. Promise me you won't do something so foolish again."

His gaze softening, Sam cupped her face. "Lucy, I'm here and I'm not going anywhere."

Lucy grabbed his shirt, fisting her hands in the fabric and shaking him. "You have to promise me not to be so reckless. I love you too much to lose you, Sam!"

Sam went still, his eyes locking on hers. "What did you just say?"

Lucy shook him again. "I said that I love you, you big igit!"

Her next words were cut off when Sam wrapped his arms around her and claimed her lips in a searing kiss. Lucy didn't bother protesting. Her emotions were running too high and she needed the reassurance of his embrace. She rose on tiptoe, kissing him back with abandon.

The way his hands roamed over her back felt so good and desire unfurled inside her. It wasn't just a physical craving, though. Her heart wanted him as much as her body did. She released his shirt, resting her palms on his chest. She whimpered in protest as he broke the kiss.

He took her face in his hands. His intense expression rendered her speechless. "I love you, too, Lucy. I love you so much, and the only reason I didn't want you learning about weapons and such was because I was afraid you'd get hurt. I couldn't bear to lose you any more than you could withstand losing me. So, if you're going to continue being angry with me for helping Josh today, I get to be angry with you."

Tears of happiness trickled from Lucy's eyes. "Do you mean it? Do you truly love me, Sam?"

He stroked her cheeks with the pads of his thumbs. "I mean every word I just said. I love you, Lucy. My heart is yours. Do you really love me?"

Lucy nodded. "Yes, Sam. I love you so much."

Sam crushed her to him, and she went eagerly into his embrace. Then she pushed against his chest, needing to settle this thing between them before giving in to the joy surging through her.

"What's wrong?" Sam asked, his breathing a little ragged.

"I don't want to fight anymore. Let's both promise each other to be as careful as we both possibly can and not to take unnecessary risks," she said.

A smile curved his lips. "I don't want to fight, either. I think your idea is a good one." He sobered a little. "But I do think you're right. It's also a good idea for you to learn to shoot better, but I want to teach you."

Lucy blinked in surprise. "You do? I thought you didn't think it was appropriate because I'm a woman."

"I realize how asinine that was of me, Lucy. How could I deny you the right to protect yourself, or other people if necessary?" Sam responded. "It would be irresponsible and cruel of me to do that. So, I want us to practice together. How does that sound to you?"

Lucy wound her arms around Sam's neck. "It sounds wonderful."

"Good." Sam kissed her cheek and whispered, "There's something else that sounds wonderful to me."

A shiver ran through her when Sam's warm breath tickled her ear. "What would that be?"

"Actually, I'd rather just show you."

Lucy laughed when he took her hand and pulled her after him, down the hall and into their room.

# EPILOGUE

*L*oud guffaws of laughter and Lucy's pretty laugh rang out across one of their fields. Several targets had been set up and Lucy and Sam's practice session had evolved into a friendly competition. Sam shook his head as he looked at the can that now lay on the ground. She'd shot it and four others off the fence in quick succession. He knew when he'd been bested.

"All right. I concede victory to my beautiful wife. I'm man enough to admit when I've lost." He dropped a kiss on her forehead. "Congratulations, my love."

"Thank you, Sam. I think I've had enough for today. I'm starving. I'll go finish supper. It won't be long until we eat, so don't dawdle in cleaning up." She gave Sam a cheeky smile and started for the house.

Sam laughed and started gathering up the various weapons they'd been practicing with. Gray and Tom helped him take the guns to the house where he locked them in a gun cabinet. He washed up and went to the kitchen where Lucy was just pulling two shepherd's pies out of the oven.

She'd already set the table and she placed the pies on the trivets that sat each end of the table. "Would you please put the bread and butter on the table, Sam?"

"Of course."

He'd just completed the task when the men came in the door. The meal commenced and Sam closed his eyes in appreciation as rich, savory flavor flooded his mouth. Lucy's excellent cooking was only one of the reasons he was blessed to be her husband. He often found himself wondering how he'd lived without her for so long.

When the meal ended, he helped her with the dishes and then they retired to the back porch. They looked out over the paddock, watching the horses in the far pasture.

"Sam, do you love me very much?"

Sam looked at Lucy. "Of course, I do. I love you more than life."

"I'm so glad. If there was more of me, would you still love me?"

A laugh escaped Sam. "Are you worried that you'll get fat for some reason? I doubt that will happen, but if it ever did, I'd still desire you as much as ever."

Lucy took his hand and kissed it. "I'm so glad to hear you say that because by February, there's going to be much, much more of me."

Shock shot up Sam's spine and he stared at her. "What are you saying, Lucy?"

Her smile was sweet and a little nervous. "I'm with child, Sam. We're going to have a baby."

How had he missed it? Looking back, he now realized that there had been no interruption of their lovemaking. He passed a hand over his face as he laughed. "Some doctor I am. I've been so wrapped up in you that I didn't realize you missed your cycle."

The blush that stained Lucy's cheek brought out a rush of love for her. "Are you happy about it?" she asked.

Taking her hands, Sam drew Lucy over onto his lap and encircled her waist with his arms. "How could I not be? I love you, and I can't wait for our baby to come."

Relief showed in her eyes as she smiled at him. "I'm so relieved. I was afraid you'd think it was too soon."

He pressed his lips to hers, enjoying their softness. "It's not too soon at all."

"I can't wait, either. We'll have to get the nursery ready before too long."

Sam chuckled and held her closer. "It'll be several months before the baby is due. We have plenty of time."

This started a good-natured argument which involved a lot of laughter. As the sunset turned into twilight, they made plans for their baby, and looked to the future with happiness and hope that the coming years would bring only good things. And if strife hit, they would face adversity together and never forget the love they'd found with one another.

The End

THANK you for reading and supporting my book and I hope you enjoyed it.

Please will you do me a favor and leave me a review It would be very much appreciated, thank you 😊

**The Rancher's Unexpected Pregnant Bride: Book 2
Excerpt**

TO LEARN MORE CLICK/TAP on a link below.
Kindle USA

Kindle UK

KINDLE CA

Kindle AUS
Blurb:

**Their age gap isn't a problem. But what she carries might ruin them both.**

Martha Walters won't chance another broken heart. But after escaping from the brothel her ex-fiancé sold her to, she believes only marriage can keep her safe. On the run and desperate to find a potential husband, she takes a risk on a handsome cattle rancher ten years her senior.

Gray Jenkins worries he's too old to attract a wife. Now in his forties, the wisecracking farmer with the soft heart takes a longshot and places an ad for a mail-order bride. But he's stunned when a charming woman a decade younger shows up on his doorstep.

As Martha falls for her gallant suitor, she's horrified to realize the secret growing in her womb could destroy their love before it starts. And despite his disbelief at his good fortune, Gray is ready to walk down the aisle until a dark enemy from Martha's past threatens to tear them apart.

Can Martha and Gray run a dangerous menace out of town to secure their happy future?

# CAST OF CHARACTERS

- **Lucy Magee**
- **Dr. Sam Slater**
- Ernie Red Dog, sheep herder
- Sheriff Josh Ryder
- Bill Eckert, owner of the Honeywell Inn
- Greta Royal, widow and housekeeper
- Mayor Delphina Stavros
- Elena, Delphina's daughter
- Reverend Paul & Annette Gibbons
- Darcy Wainwright
- Gray Jenkins, Sam's foreman
- Drake, Ernie's eldest son
- Mason & Jenny Crawford
- Robert, Drake's brother
- Grant Carlson
- Richard & Olivia Carstead

# CAST OF CHARACTERS

- Julia Simmons, midwife
- Nell, waitress at the Eatery
- Wade Bannon
- Zachariah Welliver, furniture maker
- Jensen Davis, ranch hand
- Tom Barker, ranch hand
- Eddie & Sawyer Murtaugh, brothers

# AMELIA'S OTHER BOOKS

**Montana Westward Brides series**
  #0 The Rancher's Fiery Bride
  #1 The Reckless Doctor's Bride
  #2 The Rancher's Unexpected Pregnant Bride
  #3 The Lonesome Cowboy's Abducted Bride
  #4 The Sheriff's Stubborn Secretive Bride

# CONNECT WITH AMELIA

Visit my website at **www.ameliarose.info** to view my other books and to sign up to my mailing list so that you are notified about my new releases and special offers.

# ABOUT AMELIA ROSE

Amelia is a shameless romance addict with no intentions of ever kicking the habit. Growing up she dreamed of entertaining people and taking them on fantastical journeys with her acting abilities, until she came to the realization as a college sophomore that she had none to speak of. Another ten years would pass before she discovered a different means to accomplishing the same dream: writing stories of love and passion for addicts just like herself. Amelia has always loved romance stories and she tries to tie all the elements she likes about them into her writing.

Made in the USA
Monee, IL
27 August 2020

39976721R10146